MIRACLES
IN THE
MAKING

THE KID WHISPERER:

BOOK ONE

Author: Phillip Harter

2023

Title:

Miracles in the Making

Subtitle:

Can a child find healing and recover from a world of hurt
and abuse locked up in his past memories? Find out...

Series: The Kid Whisperer, Book 1

Copyright © 2023, Phillip Harter

All rights Reserved.

ISBN: 978-1-956579-65-9

Published by: Daniel RG Crandall Publisher

PIXEL GLYPH PRESS

Design: VisualJAH

—

The contents of this book may include actual events or
sequences involving real people. The names, timeline and
details however are entirely created by the author. It is his
intent to expose and share the underlying truth of his
experiences as a child, and the transformational experience
of love and forgiveness and healing in The Kid Whisperer.

TABLE OF CONTENTS

ACKNOWLEDGEMENTS

There are so many to thank that time and space would certainly fail me to thank everyone. I will thank my Lord and Savior for His infinite tender love and care that have helped me to grow and mature into the man I am today; for being family when I didn't have or couldn't accept any other family; for the grace and mercy to save my soul and continue to nurture me when all human logic would have disdained to do so.

To my dear children...Gabrielle, Jonah, MaryAnna, Obadiah, and Gladian. There is a saying that hides in the distant shadow of my mind, refusing to the find the light just now. That saying speaks of the blows that which land so hard in the life of child that the sting can be felt by subsequent generations. This is often the story of trauma. I tried with all my being to insulate you from the trauma of my childhood. However, despite my best efforts

I know each of you have felt the sting. This reality is among the greatest regrets of my life.

You each carry such extreme value and worth from your Creator. You have each done more to bring healing and meaning into my life than you will ever know. There is so much of each of you in me, and thus so much of you in the pages of this book. I feel that everything good that I am today is because of knowing you and the healing and inspiration you have brought into my life. I love each of you more than you could possibly imagine. Thank you for being in my life.

Thank you to Junita Harter. You will never read these words, but for your choice to reach beyond your physical and mental limits to try to rescue four wild children who were desperate for anyone to stop our freefall. I understand more every day the insurmountable task that you undertook, the minimal support you were afforded, and how desperate you must have felt much of the time.

To Pat and Sandy Harter and Harry and Gladys Anderson and families who have always held an open door and an open heart even when I wasn't at all sure how to accept it or how to reciprocate. You have given me a people and a family even when I was completely ill equipped to know what to do with it.

To Betty Harter for giving me and countless others the gift of reading. You opened the door to the written word and in so doing have given me a foundational tool that I have used every day since. I sincerely hope to use this gift every remaining day with which I am blessed.

To Adam Phillips who has been by my side since I was such a wild and awkward boy. You are the kindest, gentlest soul I have ever known. I am honored to call you, my friend. Thank you for designing the cover of this work. Your eye for beauty and skill for capturing it are gifts the world is unworthy of.

As I have said, time and space would fail me, but there are so many more who have befriended and supported me through this messed up journey that has been my life. Thank you all so much. I love you all. You have become a most awkward and unusual looking family, but mine none the less.

COVER ART

I thank Adam Phillips for designing the cover, and Daniel Crandall for the final print design.

Special Thanks to Dean Worley for participating in our head shot competition for a pose on the Cover of Miracles in the Making. I sincerely appreciate his parents allowing him to participate and for being so patient with me through this long delay. Also, thanks to ACT Modeling for referring him to me.

LETTER TO THE READER:

Dear precious reader,

I am a survivor.

...A survivor of childhood physical, sexual, emotional, and psychological abuse. I spent about fourteen of my first 16 years processing in and out of the foster care system. I would receive scores of placements dealt out by officials from four different states. Ours was once called the worst case of psychological abuse in Louisiana history. We spent time in dozens of family foster homes, group homes, and even spent 18 months in a cult compound in Izard County, Arkansas.

As an adult I have been diagnosed with Post Traumatic Stress Disorder, not surprisingly, due to the complex trauma I experienced in childhood. The cumulative result of this is that my memories are shuffled, like cards before a game. They come to me in flashes and feelings that are disconnected from, or far too intense for their context today.

These memories live on within me often without any sense of chronology to give them context or definitive meaning.

However—

At the age of thirteen, I had a personal encounter with the message of Jesus Christ. This began a cascade of changes in my thinking and feeling that is still underway today.

I am no longer a throwaway kid, unwanted by the dozens of homes we visited (at least not wanted enough to adopt us), or our own parents (at least not wanted enough to do what was necessary to get us back). Now I know I am loved, valued, and highly favored by the King of the Universe. The events of my childhood are not proof of my inferiority, but rather they were simply Miracles in the Making. Each trauma, each setback, each rejection, and struggle represent its own chance for God to demonstrate His love and power in my life; to teach me how to take back control of my own emotions and grow to experience the peace and love He has for me! Time and time again, over the past 40 years he has demonstrated His love and power in very real and tangible ways.

Then, in 2019 my wife of 19 1/2 years made the decision to begin the process of dissolving our marriage. This sent Shockwaves through our home and effectively ended the church ministry that had been my world for my entire adult life.

Here I was at 39, my family torn apart, my career over, my home lost, betrayed by the person I thought was my best friend. My kids are my everything; and for the first time in their lives, I was away from them, and not a little. For nearly two years my relationship with them was reduced to maybe spending four days a month with them. While I was away from them, three of my kids received major, potentially life altering diagnosis. Three of them had to have surgery. All of their academics began to flounder, and I was virtually helpless to do anything about any of it.

These events woke me out of my complacent sleep, shook me to my very core, and gave me time and motivation to meditate, taking stock of the things that are important in my life. They returned me from the virtual fantasy world I'd been living in, to the world where there is pain that threatens to completely overtake, anger that is virtually unbearable, and always someone there on the other side to comfort you when the only thing left to do is cry. My very reality was threatening to tailspin.

What I found through this was that when my faith was challenged most, my best friend was more than sufficient to catch me when I fell. (And believe me, I fell hard.) I soon felt my focus return to a deep-seated desire, that I feared was gone forever; to yield my voice and my life to the broken and hurting.

Can faith hold up when the bottom falls out of your life? Where is God when bad, even unspeakably bad things happen? Can faith have an answer to depression when it comes on like waves of the sea at storm surge threatening to take you under indefinitely? Does abandonment ever abandon its victims? Does church or faith really have the answers to any of these questions? During the past few years, I have been forced to face each of these questions and more.

"How did they come out?" you ask. Well, I do want to address some of them with you; but... I have more in common with hurting kids than I do almost anyone else. They are my tribe and most of these questions were originally answered in my own early adult life. These answers came as I tried to navigate the aftermath of my own childhood trauma—like a Nascar driver trying to pull his car out of a complete spin while avoiding the rest of the field, or the kids from "Space Camp" trying to regain control of their shuttle and set the proper course before they burned up on reentry. That's how my early adult life was.

I had to hurry up and figure out as much as possible about life before it slammed me in the face. Pretty much all I gained from the examples of adults in my life was a whole lot of what not to do. However, I learned a long time ago that my exposures and experiences during my childhood are not weaknesses, but rather are that which God eventually used to give me the unique perspective that has helped me through everything since, even of late.

Since our American paradise (which seems so picturesque on its surface) often hides some truly ugly and devastating realities—the victims of which usually have no voice at all; and the need to combat such realities and love their victims through a healing journey are so great—it just makes a ton of sense to relate the truths that have carried me through by presenting them to you as they once were to me—in the context and aftermath of childhood trauma.

I began writing at age 13. when I started my first novel. I wrote about sixty to eighty pages before the manuscript was lost. I would begin novels again in high-school, college, and after college; but each project would somehow become damaged or inaccessible.

In 2019, when I entered the season that totally rocked my world, my faith, my confidence, my very identity was in jeopardy. However, God is still faithful. Soon I knew it was time to write again. In September of 2020, like many of you, I was laid off from my job (for the third time that year) and began The Kid Whisperer series—a project which you're now tasting the first morsels of.

What comes after this is a work of fiction. Or, it's a glimpse into a parallel universe that runs so near our own, that hopefully the emotions and ideas will slide easily between the two, bringing you, beloved, to a place of reflection and meditation, providing a spring board for you to answer questions you never thought to ask, and take actions you never dared imagine. This life cannot be summed up by our past or even our present, but by how that past and this present catapult us into a better future!

This book may be something you bought, but the message within is a gift from my most special friend. I hope and pray that you get to know Him for the first time, or just get to know Him better in the pages to come.

Thanks for reading. Now, look-out for your own Miracles in the Making.

THE HIDING PLACE

10/13/2023

4:35 PM

Jeff pulled his jacket tighter, trying to fit his whole frame inside. He calmed down and noticed the cold rain on his cheeks as it mingled with his hot tears. He shivered in his hiding place, tracing the raw skin around the wound on his face. He winced as he touched the lump forming on his forehead. The physical pain was minor compared to the sadness and fear that overwhelmed him, burning like a fireball in his chest; giving rise to the spontaneous bursts of tears that ended with him gasping for air and whimpering under his breath.

Perhaps most 8-year-olds would have been afraid here, alone in the dim light; but Jeff felt safe within the high metal walls. He was certain he'd chosen his hiding place well.

His heart was heavy, and his mind raced as he crouched in momentary safety. He knew that if he ever went home his stepdad would kill him. He thought back to the violent events of the day...

When Mama cried, he always hid in the closet, in the tiny space behind his toy box. He would stay there until he heard the front door close, or until Mama came to get him.

This time was different. Instead of being frozen in fear, his mind kept creating ideas of things *he* could do ...to get away, to help. At first, he squeezed his eyes tight, forcing them from his mind. Too afraid to think about them for more than an instant.

Finally, without settling on any real plan, he slipped from his hidey hole and dashed for the center of his room. He crouched on the floor and peeked through the partially open door. He could see his mother lying on the floor just beyond where the hallway opened into the dining room. That's where he saw Jim standing over her.

"Stay down!" He yelled, cursing, "Just stay down!" He yelled the expletive with such force it seemed to land as its own blow. The movement in his mother's arm was faint and barely perceivable, but Jim erupted in a barrage of kicks to her stomach and side.

That's when Jeff snapped. He was a tiny frame. He might have weighed sixty pounds soaking wet; but he lowered his head, ran as fast as he could, driving his head into Jim's thigh. The sound Jeff uttered began as some kind of hybrid between a primal growl and a yell gaining strength and ferocity as if it was escaping from some hidden prison within the child and until it possessed him, **"UGGGH! STOP HURTING MY MOM!"**

His attempt was futile, though spirited.

The reaction was instant. The force of Jeff's attempt was enough to make the big man take a small step backwards as Jeff bounced off. This gave Jim just enough room. He drew back his right arm and swung it with all of his might catching Jeff right on the chin with the back of his hand. Something on Jim's hand or wrist, a watch or ring tore the boy's face. With the force, the boy's light frame lifted easily off the ground and was propelled across the dining room. Nothing left of the strength that threatened the big man's balance an instant ago.

Jeff landed hard on his left shoulder and slid across the wood floor. His head struck the wall about two inches above the baseboard shattering the drywall and finding something solid beneath. Jeff felt himself begin to freeze, but the sound of Jim stomping towards him somehow snapped him free. He looked up.

The look of sheer rage on the big man's face filled Jeff's own heart with a terror that he had never known before Jim came into their lives.

Jeff scrambled to his feet and ran through the screen door.

"You little—" more cursing, "I'm gonna kill you! Get back here! You're finally gonna get what the hell you deserve!" Jim boomed.

Jeff reached the edge of the yard, but when he turned back he saw his stepfather's huge frame coming through the screen door.

The front yard did not give Jeff much of a head start, but he took full advantage. Panic filling his heart and mind; he ran as hard as he possibly could, pumping his arms and legs with all his might. He cut through the neighbor's yard, and into the alley. Jeff's eyes seemed disconnected from his mind as he ran. He was driven solely by terror and he had no thought of where he was or even where he'd been. He did not look back, certain the slightest hesitation would leave him feeling Jim's huge hands on his hair or shoulders. Jim loved to yank him around with his scruffy blond hair. Or forcefully guide him with huge hands that squeezed his shoulders tight enough to leave dark purple bruises where the pad of his fingers and thumb dug in.

Jeff crossed several streets and made several more turns before he entered an alley. His legs were aching terribly, he was soaking wet from the mix of sweat and pouring rain; his heart pounded in his chest. The rage that drove him from his hidey hole had quickly been replaced by sheer terror that had fueled his determined refusal to be caught. The terror now gradually faded as cognition returned to his mind and exhaustion crept into his limbs. He again ran, arriving halfway down the alley before he stopped to turn around. He expected to see the big man there. To his surprise, he was alone.

He immediately scanned for a place to hide. His eyes fell on a dumpster just ahead. There was a wood pallet leaning against the side. He carefully climbed the pallet, raised the plastic lid, and peered inside. He was aware for the first time of the pain in his shoulder. The dumpster was surprisingly empty given the steady rain. Just then a ground-shaking thunder bolt sealed his decision. He hopped down letting the lid close as a protection above him.

Now he could feel his warm tears mixing with the cold rain on his cheeks. Sharp pain seemed to streak like the blood from his face and forehead where he'd hit the wall. His right cheek bled, and he could now feel the dull pain of a bruise forming on his chin.

Jeff had no way to know how long he was in the dumpster. His heart had slowed. His head cleared, and his mind presented him with new, unanswered questions: chiefly, what was he going to do now? No answers would come to him. He just hoped so hard that Jim wouldn't find Him.

Jim was the meanest man Jeff had ever known. He'd always hated Jeff, but today was the first time Jeff had dared to fight back. The lump in his throat grew and he cried harder as he faced the fact that Jim would surely kill him if he ever went home...

How would he even find his way home?

Suddenly, Jeff snapped to attention. Movement above him! He sought out the sound with his eyes.

The roof-door creaked. He jerked his head up to see what was happening. As he did, he slammed the back of his head against the medal wall sending pain ringing inside his head as the sound rang out.

Panic struck, as a man's face appeared. He instinctively jumped to the opposite corner of the small space as a new and terrifying fact appeared to him. In his panic he'd climbed the pallet and jumped into the dumpster. But now he was caught. There was no way out!

The sudden sound of the man's voice fed his fear.

"Oh! Hey there fella, I didn't mean to scare ya." He said, disappearing as quickly as he had appeared. Jeff couldn't see him now, but this voice was low and level, and the man's his face was kind, though the shock *was* evident.

A few moments later he reappeared. "Hey, wanna get out of there?"

Jeff pressed his back hard against the far side of the dumpster, shaking his head. Terror was on the boy's face.

The man once again disappeared and instead a boy appeared.

"Hey, my friend, thought you might need a hand?" The boy said in an upbeat tone, a huge smile on his face. The boy looked at Jeff, and the toe of his tennis shoe appeared on the brim of the dumpster.

"It's ok, mind if I come in?" he asked. Hopping over the wall, he jumped inside without waiting for a response. "I'm Cole. I brought you something."

Cole was wearing bright blue jeans, a royal blue jacket, and tennis shoes, which were slightly dirty but still white. However, Jeff's eyes went straight to the McDonald's bag in his hand. Suddenly he felt very hungry.

Cole seemed to read his mind. "I got some chicken nuggets left, if ya want 'em."

Jeff felt his muscles soften as he nodded, grabbing the bag as it was offered, and tearing it open. He watched for the man to return as he began eating. He had finished the first nugget when he remembered. "Thanks," he said, glancing at Cole.

Cole was about his own age, maybe a little younger—but not much, with dark black hair. His face and eyes seemed to dance, always smiling.

Jeff instantly liked him.

Silence rested on the scene for a few moments as Jeff chewed the nuggets.

Finally, Cole asked in a soft voice, "So, what are you doing in here, anyways?"

As Jeff chewed the rest of his nugget, the gash on the side of his face seemed to wink at Cole.

The rest of Jeff's face was a mess too—with the winking gash extending from just above the boy's right cheekbone and down to his jaw. There was a lump obviously rising from the left side of his forehead, and the dark, matted blood contrasted against his wet, towhead scruff. The green and black camo pants he wore seemed to grow right out of the bottom of his blue jacket when he stood up. His black and white tennis shoes were so worn that on both feet a sockless big toe could be seen poking out of one side.

"I was running away" Jeff answered in a quiet voice and looking at the rusty metal floor.

A brief pause let the words settle, "You must be pretty brave then. Most of us are too scared to run away," Cole said. His voice was high pitched and happy, but his eyes seemed to say more than his words. They softened and seemed to focus more now, a sad understanding unconsciously reaching out to comfort his new friend.

Jeff noticed the word "us" and felt Instinctively that Cole understood. But how?

The confusion was on his face and Cole picked it up easily. "Hey," Cole paused, "Why don't you come with us? I know you're scared, but could going with us really be scarier than being in this dumpster when it gets dark? We'll get you some dry clothes. If you don't wanna stay after you check it out, we can bring you back. Bill is a good man. He's nice and he helps kids like us," Cole explained.

Jeff thought for several minutes. He imagined the cold dumpster after dark, as a shiver involuntarily rocked his whole frame. He was soaked clear through his clothes, and what if the next face he saw was Jim's? The hair on the back of his neck stood up as the shiver was chased by a shutter of terror that ran from the base of his head the full length of his body. The thought of Jim peering down on him, trapped here. His mind refused to imagine what would happen next.

"Ok." He said, his voice barely carrying a hint of the desperation he felt.

As if on cue, Bill's voice boomed cheerily from outside. "Cole, you guys ok in there?"

"Yeah, I think we're about ready to get out of here. Can you give us a hand?" Cole asked.

"Thought you'd never ask," Bill returned, sliding the wood pallet over the side for the boys to climb up on.

Cole climbed up first, took Bill's hand, and jumped to the ground. Jeff hesitantly followed, careful to avoid raising his injured shoulder high enough to feel the shot of pain that would follow.

As he reached the top, he felt the older man scanning his face.

Something in Bill's eyes seemed to ease the fear that Jeff felt. grabbing Bill's hand, he jumped to the ground. He used the strong and steady hand to anchor his landing as he jumped from the high dumpster wall.

Bill

"I'm Bill," he said, hoping the boy would reveal his own name, it worked.

"I'm Jeff."

"Hey Jeff, it's nice to meet you." Bill began. "I've put in a call to the authorities, and they said it's ok for you to come with us. They'll send someone to check on you a little later. First, how about some more nuggets, then we'll head home for some dry clothes?"

"Ok." Jeff said hesitantly, slowly nodding his head. He followed Cole into the big van.

Earlier in the Van

3:52 PM

Bill looked at the boy in the passenger's seat in sheer amazement. Cole is so bright, so brilliant. He's witty, smart, and radiant with positivity...a true miracle in the making, right there! The thought brought his eyes to the small white sign posted on the dash. It read "Miracles in the Making." It was the theme of *The Home*—the theme of Bill's very life.

As his eyes returned to the road, he saw in his mind the terrified, nearly catatonic boy he'd met just six short months ago. Bill could hardly imagine that this boy had lain in a fetal position in the closet of a party house where four bodies were found overdosed with methamphetamines.

2

MIRACLES IN THE MAKING

Bill's thoughts went back to the events of March 2023…

Six Months earlier

The coroner estimated that the victims had been deceased at least 3 days due to the level of decomposition. Since they were presumed to have been alive when Cole went into the closet, it's estimated that he was in there 4 to 6 days without food or water, listening to the sounds of his sister being physically and sexually abused. He too had been tooled for their sick uses before becoming too weak to continue and tossed aside to die alone in the dark.

Kids are utterly amazing in their level of resilience. Although Bill honestly gave the glory to God for each of these kids that he was able to see bounce back from depths and varieties of trauma that would destroy most adults.

Truly the only comparison to the kind of traumatic abuse that these kids go through in the adult world are POW's, Prisoners of War! These men and women are tortured and abused for weeks, months, or worse. Even with the extreme training that our heroes on the front lines receive, a few weeks in a POW camp can break the best and toughest of men. Bill thought, "We get kids that have been subjected to as bad or worse, often *for years*. The fact that any survive, much less *bounce back* is a miracle in the truest sense of the word!"

Bill remembered the call from Chief Taylor asking him to come. The chief was sure they would have to take the boy to the hospital, but he wanted to give Bill a crack first...."no that's not right." Bill corrected his own thought. "We wanted to give God a crack first. That's who was doing the work. Everything was Him." Bill thought about all that had happened.... the founding of *The Home*, the rescue of so many kids. It was one miracle after another, after another, after another. He honestly just felt honored to be a part of it.

Bill isn't just a part of it. He's the heart of it. It is what God has done in his own heart to give him that special level of sensitivity and intuition about kids and trauma that make The Home such a special place. It is Bill's experiences and unique gifts that serve as God's toolbox in this miraculous, healing work.

He continued to think back to March…

The child looked to be about Six or Seven years old. He hadn't spoken a word since he had been picked up at the crime scene. It's not merely the scene of *the crime* or of *a* crime. Too many crimes were committed in that place! Four bodies in total had been recovered from the small two-bedroom house.

"Jack" was found curled in a fetal position on the floor of a bedroom closet. His soiled shorts were the only clothes he wore. Authorities had yet to identify the skinny, black headed, dark-skinned boy who wore the blank stare. They had just nick-named him "Jack" until he could be identified later. They could be sure of nothing, but they didn't think he lived at 413 Commerce Street, the address that police were given when neighbors made the complaint: The unmistakable and very repulsive odor of rotting flesh.

The house had been occupied by two methamphetamine addicts believed not to have children. Well, actually they had four children between the two of them, all of whom had been removed from the home, parental rights terminated, and placed for adoption.

It would take the Baymont Police Department a while to sort out exactly what happened. The only person who may have witnessed anything wasn't talking.

"Jack" arrived at police headquarters at about half past four. A call had been made from the scene to Bill Hinchum, the operator of an incredibly unique shelter called "Home" If you read his organizational documents, you'd find the words "Now and Forever" tacked on, but everyone knew it as "Home." (Now and Forever Home)

Bill had built an incredibly special place. The campus held several very large "houses." One was called "Now House." This is the emergency shelter that was operated by Home. The others where called "Forever House" and "And Ever House." These were the adoptive houses for the kids that had been adopted by Mr. Hinchum officially, and his entire staff unofficially.

There were two more, yet unnamed, houses under construction. They were for the "fall back kids." Meaning they were for the kids that returned after being out in the world. This was not a "children's home" or a "foster home" Both of these terms represent something temporary, isolating, and sterile; absent of the one thing kids need almost above all, love. This was a real forever home. Instead of forbidding permanent, familiar connections, and living in a constant state of anticipation for the dissolution of all ties, here there was a lifelong commitment from day one. The focus was on building things that would last a lifetime. These kids would come back for holidays, help, or rest; for the rest of their lives just as any child might return home to visit his or her parents.

Mr. Hinchum arrived at the station shortly after the police brought Jack in. He saw Jack in a little interview room just off the waiting area and accompanied by a secretary. (Bill had requested that the boy not be left alone) When Bill entered the room he was carrying what looked like a picnic basket. He came in and quietly took a seat across from the boy. Without saying a word, he opened the basket. He reached in and removed a plastic platter, a plastic bowl with a lid and small bottles of barbecue sauce and ketchup. After he placed the platter on the table, he opened the plastic bowl and poured out enough chicken nuggets and fries to pile up in the center and nearly overflow the platter. He then placed it in the center of the table. Next, he squirted catchup, and barbecue sauce into two small cups that he pulled from his basket. Finally, he retrieved two 16 oz. bottles of Sprite. One of them he set on the table in front of Jack.

Then He looked at Jack for the first time. Hi, someone said they are calling you Jack,"That's kind of a funny name. Mine's Bill, and it's a bit funny too." I'm going to close my eyes for a few short minutes, and then I'm going to eat some chicken nuggets and fries, and I'm going to drink my Sprite. It's not nice to eat in front of people, so I brought enough for you. You can have as much as you want.

Bill

I closed my eyes in prayer. A few moments later I opened them to see Jack, a very skinny, Black headed boy with dark eyes and long, black eyelashes. He was a striking character. A good-looking kid even though he was filthy. The little red shorts he was wearing were not even visible beneath the table. What was almost visible—almost thick enough to taste—was the smell. The boy had clearly soiled the shorts multiple times over an extended period. The ammonia of urine burned my nostrils, but I had learned to ignore such things.

When I opened my eyes, the young man was shoveling chicken nuggets into his mouth like a kid throwing ski-balls into a machine at the arcade …if he had put a token in two machines side by side, his right arm was engaged in a race with his left arm to see which one could throw the most balls before the time ran out. That's exactly what I thought of when I opened my eyes. Right before I acknowledged that he probably hadn't eaten in days.

The secretary, I noticed, still sitting in the corner of the room, was dumbfounded. Her jaw was fully extended as if it were giving its best effort to reach the floor. She seemed to be modeling for "Jack" how to get the most into his own mouth. I took no more notice of her.

I saw how fast he was eating, after the ski ball vision, I had two thoughts almost simultaneously. First, I thought he's going to empty the platter before I ever get one. The second was Its time to bring out reinforcements.

I reached into my basket and retrieved the two other butter tubs filled with nuggets and fries. "I promise, I have plenty, and you really can have as much as you want." I began to eat. Watching carefully to notice his response.

Jack noticed the two bowls and his eyes rose to meet mine, but he only met my gaze for an instant.

It didn't take me long to notice, he wasn't slowing down. Considering his small frame and the number of nuggets he had already consumed, I figured if I didn't move things along the current blend of aroma would be joined by that of vomit. I quietly reached into my basket and withdrew two small styrofoam bowls of strawberry Ice cream and a couple of plastic spoons. When I saw the recognition on the boy's face, I seized my opportunity to try to get him talking.

Without looking at him, I asked, "should I call you Jack, or is there another name that you like to be called?"

The boy seemed to freeze in place staring at me for a long time as if considering whether or not to respond.

I kept myself busy opening the ice cream; glancing at him only for a second to try to spur him on, but avoiding making eye contact.

"It— It's c— c— Cole." The boy began slowly and quietly. He seemed to be trying to find his voice as if he hadn't used it in a very long time."

"Well Cole, it's nice to meet you." I began (lowering my voice to match Cole's volume keenly aware of my cadence). "Do you like ice cream? I seem to have brought an extra." I said, looking at one of my cups of ice cream as if I was genuinely confused.

"Y— Yes sir, I do," Cole stuttered again, still noticeably nervous, but clearly more secure this time. I sat the opened bowl on the table in front of Cole along with a plastic spoon. Next, I turned my focus to my own dessert, leaving space for the boy to speak without drawing my attention to him.

I noticed his face soften ever so slightly. His thick black eyebrows still hung low, and his expression was tight. It was clear he had the weight of the world on his shoulders and pretty heavy storm clouds on his face too.

If you spend much time with kids, especially those that have been traumatized, then you know they will sometimes have a whole spring thunderstorm take up residence right there on their face. And if you look, you can see something powerful brewing underneath. I've seen a whole lot of kids through the years with storm clouds on their faces. Sometimes the clouds bring rain, but other times, when things were really bad; they don't. (Not that I'd ever rule it out, but if the boy in front of me had been a little older, I'd have expected his storm to bring anger. Time would tell. I had a fairly good hunch that this was going to be one of those really bad times. I was careful to remind myself that I'd need to take it very slow with Cole.

(Bill remembered he could tell that day at the station that this young man was in a very dark hole, and as usual, he would take it upon himself to lead him out. That's what he always did. He always walks into every situation as if he is the only hope for the child or children that he meets. It's the reason he is now the first call the police or social services make any time the situation is really bad. Not because He thinks that way, but because he's that good. Bill had a pretty bad childhood himself, so he feels that he has a sense about kids, and over the years it has become clear to everyone that he does.)

The ice cream was nearly gone, so I figured it was time to close the sale. I pulled my phone from my pocket.

"Cole, I want to show you a video,"

I slowly slid my phone across the table and pushed play on the video. The video gave a very thorough tour of Now Home. The video showed two boys—Timmy, 7, and Zeek, 8 years old—walking through the house, pointing out everything that a visitor might need to know, or just be curious about in order to feel at home. Timmy also took time, tears in his eyes, to assure any potential visitor that it was, "—a really good place, that changes everything, really! It does. I promise!"

When the video was ended, Cole's eyes rose to meet mine and I could see tears being held back. "Cole, would you like to spend the night at this home? We don't have to talk tonight if you don't want to. You can meet the other kids if you want to, but you don't have to. I'll give you clean clothes. You can wear them or not." I really hoped and expected that he would. "You can take a bath, or not. You can have more chicken nuggets and ice cream before bed if you like, and Ms. Debra will make you whatever you want for breakfast in the morning. After that we can talk and see what you want to do."

Cole had been really skittish with his eyes since they found him. Not making eye contact with anyone except for the glances he'd given me. He had spoken to no one until I arrived. Now I could see the tears were now welling up there. Yep, that dam was about to break. I moved around the table as quickly as I dared without affecting the progression of events.

Cole was nodding, but he was breaking. I knelt beside him making my shoulder, the perfect landing zone for his tear-streaked face. I patted him on the shoulders and waited for a long time for him to cry, fighting back my own tears when I considered what he must be feeling. I was a complete stranger to him, yet something in this little exchange made him comfortable enough to respond this way.

Kids are resilient and so much tougher than they should ever have to be. However, I was aware that, like a sponge, they can often only soak up so much water before needing to be wrung out. The amount of time he lasted was a credit to his courage. As I felt his sobs subside, I just gathered him up, and headed for the van.

I've been told that I violated any number of boundaries with these kids, but my approach is to be trauma aware, and trauma informed; not trauma controlled. Children need love. If I were standing with an adult that was breaking down, I would offer them my shoulder and even pat their shoulders to comfort them. It would be innocent and a direct response to their expressed need. I always thought it was ridiculous to do differently with a child who desperately needs the safety and comfort of a healthy embrace in these moments.

The paperwork was all done when I arrived, before I entered the room. I was prepared, but since I welcomed my first boy, I've always tried to let it be their decision whether or not to come with me.

I knew I'd have to take it slow. We had no idea, and in hindsight, could not have imagined what this child had been through in the past few days. Why in the world would he trust some random stranger? Every situation is different, but there is a process to gaining a kid's trust. *That trust is a sacred honor. Not to be violated!*

—

The secretary who was still sitting in the corner, quietly shook her head. She'd never seen Bill work before. It hugely impressed her. How could a man—and one so big and broad—be so tender and have such an instinct about the needs of such a fragile child. It was a mystery to her. As she watched him leave, a certain admiration for this man grew within her.

Stan, a member of *The Home Crew*, sat in the little Baymont Police Department waiting room. As Bill emerged from the interview room carrying the boy, he quickly stood up and went outside to bring the van. He had seen this a few times now, but it still never ceased to amaze him. "I work for the Kid Whisperer," he had observed long ago. Now that thought repeated every time the awe of a scene like this would overwhelm him. "Somehow, he is able to understand exactly what these kids need to remove their fears and reach their hearts. Sometimes they are crying, other times they might be screaming and cussing and ready to tear down the entire world with their bare hands. It doesn't seem to matter. Bill Henham has a way." He thought, quietly shaking his head and smiling as he fired up the engine.

When Bill walked Cole to the double side doors of the van, Stan had already placed a child booster at the end of the bench seat right behind the driver. Bill sat Cole on his feet in the parking lot and opened the door, and the two climbed in.

"Cole this is Stan, he's very nice, and he'll be driving us tonight."

Stan nodded and smiled at Cole who barely looked at him, careful not to make eye contact.

3

COMING HOME

Back in the Van Before Jeff

Today, 10/13/23

4:35 PM

Bill shook himself free of the memories and smiled at the boy beside him now. He was driving the van away from McDonald's after leaving the courthouse. Cole was eating chicken nuggets, but his movements were slow and distracted. It was a surprise on their way home from his adoption hearing, a throwback to that first night in the station.

The court just granted Bill's adoption of Cole. It was fitting that it would be final on the half year anniversary of his coming home that first time.

Cole's cheeks were plump and smooth now. His eyes were free of the paralyzing fear. Gone were the fading bruises and dark circles beneath his eyes that had clouded his face the night Bill had first met him.

He looked like a different child, his eyes bright and clear as he munched the nuggets now. Bill knew, despite the boy's peaceful demeanor, his trauma was not gone. It was no longer the raging tsunami that seemed sure to destroy him that first night, but it was no more gone than the waves of the sea. Today those waves were a gentle surf, but the power and pain of that past trauma would bring more storms to Cole's shores, the thought Bill knew all too well. A hint of fear rose in the man's own heart. His only reassurance was that Cole would not face those storms alone. The decision of the court today meant that Cole would always have Bill and the others from *The Home* there to help and support him when that monster chose to bare his ugly head again.

Bill figured they'd finished about half of the twenty-piece. He didn't want to leave them in the van while they were at the bowling alley (the second part of Cole's celebratory surprise), so he'd pull down the next little alley to toss them in a dumpster.

Bill leapt out of the van and approached the dumpster. He reached for the plastic lid with his right hand, grateful that it was unlocked. The McDonald's bag was in his left hand; but before he could toss it in: he dropped the bag on the ground. It's the only reason he slowed down enough to hear the clang above the sound of the steady rain. Expecting an animal, and hoping for something cool to show Cole, he opened the dumpster, and peered in... To his complete shock, there was a kid!

The child looked terrified, shivering, and looked pretty badly roughed up.

Bill tried to reassure him, "Hey there fella, I didn't mean to scare you." Bill said, but he could see his eyes widen. The child was becoming more frightened by the second.

Bill sought to offer the boy help out but wasn't surprised when he shook his head. He turned around and returned to the driver's door that hung open.

"Hey Cole, there's a kid trapped in this dumpster. He's in bad shape. He's really scared. Do you think you could talk to him?" Bill's words came slow and clear, his voice was low, but there was an urgency that was unmistakable.

Bill has created a culture of helping at *The Home*, and Cole has spent the past 6 months being encouraged by other boys with parallel paths. However, Bill was also very aware that Cole's own trauma had left with a nearly phobic fear of both tight spaces, and the dark. His response would be a testament to his growth and of his seemingly endless capacity for compassion and empathy.

"Sure, " Cole offered. Bill lifted him onto the pallet, and Cole took over from there....

As soon as Cole leapt into the dumpster, Bill was on the phone with Chief.

"Hello, Chief?" He expected the chief to answer since it was his personal cell.

"Yes, Bill, what's up?"

"David, I need your approval. I stopped over here to throw away some trash in a dumpster in the alley behind Halifax Street. Yeah anyway, we found a kid trapped in here. He's very shook up and has some potentially serious injuries. Definitely been physically assaulted. Think it would be OK to take him for a home visit, try to see what happened?" Bill inquired.

It was probably not how most jurisdictions would have handled such events, but these two had been working together for a long time. Trust had grown between them, slow and strong like an Oak. And, like one of the huge oaks on the property of *The Home*, that trust had weathered many a storm.

"Do you think he needs medical attention?" was the question chief asked, his voice going distant the way it did when his mind was in motion. He wanted to ask how the hell a little boy could be in a dumpster and his parents not be turning the who damn world upside down looking for him, but he had seen enough to know that not everyone was a civilized human being.

"He's stable for the moment. I'll have to get him cleaned up and get a better look at him to know for sure. He'll for sure need some first aid for his cuts and ice for his head. I can get an assessment and let you know."

"Sure Bill. I'll start everything on this end. I'll get Susie on the line and have her get things going too. If he needs medical attention, of course that will accelerate our time line. I don't have to tell you to document. Call me when you know more, we'll come by tonight or in the morning to put eyes on him," Answered Chief Taylor

"Will do. Thanks Chief."

"Bill..." chief paused. The thought came out before he could anticipate the response. "...How the heck did he pick the dumpster you were gonna visit?"

"Must be The Lord, Dave. Must be the Lord!" Bill had already whispered a prayer for this miracle.

Chief simply exhaled deeply as the line went dead.

Bill couldn't see Chief of Police, David Taylor, but if he could, he knew he'd be doing his patented head shake. He always did that when there was something he couldn't wrap his mind around. Bill hoped one day he'd have the faith to accept that God really does intervene in the affairs of men. Bill sure had seen it a lot in his work with kids. In the meantime, Bill was glad, once again, that his friend would have to step over a pretty obvious miracle to deny it.

Bill returned to stand beside the dumpster following his phone call.

"Hey Cole, you guys ok in there?" Bill shouted, trying to keep his voice pleasant as he added volume.

Cole answered in the affirmative, and let Bill know they were ready to get out.

Bill quickly raised the pallet over his head and lowered it down the inside of the dumpster. Cole jumped out first. As the new boy climbed up, Bill scanned his injuries. He had a pretty ugly gash on his face, some bruises, a goose egg on his head and blood in his hair. He'd have to see how deep that gash was, if that bump was bleeding, and if he had any other physical injuries that were less obvious. However, it looked like these injuries could be treated at Home. It was the other injuries that would be the most difficult to treat.

As careful as Bill was to notice the boy's outward injuries, he also paid close attention to his eyes. He noticed the fear there was still evident, though it was noticeably less than before.

"Dear God," he thought, "What horrors have happened to this boy today? Thank you for bringing him to us. Please help us help him."

A thought, a silent voice seemed to answer, "I already have."

Bill knew He referred to his last request to help us help him. Yes, He had already helped us help him, but he had a feeling there would be much more helping to be done.

"I'm Bill", he said as the boy, visibly terrified and soaked to the bone, took his hand to jump down. His intent was to get the boy to reveal his own name without feeling like he was being interrogated. It worked.

"I'm Jeff." His answer was tentative, but his voice was clear.

These words brought a smile to Bill's face. The Lord had already given so much courage to this boy, granting Bill favor in his sight, so he could trust him at least enough to share his name.

Obviously, the second part of Cole's surprise was postponed since he and Bill had picked up their new passenger.

As soon as the boys were loaded in the van, Bill thought of Jeff's wet clothes and the large lump forming on his forehead. He reached up to turn down the blower on the heater, but he did not increase the temperature. He knew his new charge was cold, but he didn't want him to get too warm and go to sleep either just in case he had a concussion.

From the Back Seat

Today, 4:52 PM

Shortly after the van started moving towards Home, Jeff leaned over slightly towards Cole.

"What did you mean, Kids like us?" he asked in a voice barely audible.

Cole looked at his new friend and whispered too..."6 months ago Bill saved me from some really bad stuff." When we get Home, you will see a lot of kids he's saved."

"The funny thing is...I got chicken nuggets when I met him too," Cole said as he passed Jeff a six piece from Bill as the van sat at the McDonald's drive-through window.

"Wow!" Jeff exclaimed as he accepted the food. His eyes darted at Bill and then at Cole. His voice was low, with a tone of disbelief. His eyes were wide with surprise. "Thanks".

As the boys began to munch their nuggets and the van returned to motion, Cole's curiosity could no longer be contained. He wanted to know what had happened to his new friend. As he began to speak, his voice was low and hesitant, allowing the empathy to ooze between the words. "You don't have to say, but what happened to you anyways." His smile had faded to genuine concern now.

"My stepdad. He's the meanest man in the world!" Jeff said in a low sheepish tone, touching the wound on his face.

"But how?" Cole asked.

"I was trying to help my mom. He was kicking her." Jeff said, thinking of his mom. "I don't know what happened really. I just got so mad. I rushed him."

"Wow! I knew you were brave," Cole said.

"It didn't work." He said abruptly keeping his volume low with something between self-defeat and disappointment there. Clearly he did not feel he had been brave. "I couldn't stop him. He just swatted me away like a bug." Jeff said, tears in his eyes.

"Hey! At least you didn't just hide in the closet!" Cole said, staring at the floor. "I guess I'm just a chicken." His tone was reassuring before trailing off at the end.

"That's what I always did before." Jeff said. "I never did anything else before except hide in my closet."

"Closets are the safest sometimes! So, what happened when you rushed him?" Cole asked.

"He hit me. I flew like a stuffed animal!" Jeff said.

"Oh! Wow! That must have hurt like crazy!"

"I went right through the wall. My head hurts pretty bad." He said touching the goose egg on his forehead.

"Whoa! That's crazy. You could have died!" Cole exclaimed. "How did you get away?"

"I don't know. He was chasing me, but I just kept on running. Finally, I jumped in that dumpster." Jeff explained.

"Wow! I can't believe you ran away! That's crazy! You're so brave. I don't think I could have done that. I was way too scared. I just froze and laid there in the closet. I didn't even know that three people died while I was in there." Cole said.

"Three people died?" Jeff exclaimed, "Ah man, that's bad. That might have been worse than Jim " Jeff said, his voice trailing off. He wondered if his mom was dead. Warm tears escaped his eyes. He tried to wipe them away with his fists, but they ran down his face streaking the dirt and blood that was already dried there.

Cole quietly reached into a pouch in the back of the seat in front of him and pulled out a box of tissues. He handed Jeff the box.

Jeff pulled one out and wiped the streaking tears from his cheeks wincing as he brushed his sore face, the wound already stung from the salt in his tears. He dropped the box on the seat beside him.

Jeff felt Cole looking at him. He raised his head and looked at his new friend. He could see tears welling up in Cole's eyes too. The sad look there mirrored his own hurt and something shifted deep inside. For the first time in a very long time, he began to understand that he wasn't alone.

"I wish I was as brave as you. My sister almost died, because I was too scared to even try to help." Cole said, pulling his own tissue now to wipe the tears from his own cheeks.

"My mom might have died today, because I waited too long, and I wasn't big enough." Jeff said.

The boys sat in silence for a few minutes dabbing their eyes before turning their attention to the four remaining nuggets in the box.

"Chicken nuggets are my favorite!" Cole said, his smile lighting up his face again.

"Me too!" Jeff said flashing a grin that faded quickly to a wince from the pain in his face.

"Hey Cole," Came Bill's gentle voice from the driver's seat. "We're going to be pulling in here in a sec. How do you feel about spending another night at Now House?" Bill asked from the front seat.

"Why..." Cole's voice trailed as he answered his own question.

"What's Now House?" Jeff asked quietly directing his question only to Cole.

"It's the most amazing and magical place ever!" Cole exclaimed excitedly. "When they brought me here, I was so scared I was almost dead."

"What?" Jeff asked, honestly amazed.

"Yeah. I couldn't talk or anything. I barely knew where I was. I wasn't doing good at all." Cole explained. "I felt like I was falling. Like I would never stop. Bill was so good; the people here were so nice." He stretched the word so for emphasis. "I have never been around people like this. It was like they caught me. Now I get to stay, forever."

Bill looked in the visor mirror as Jeff's eyes lowered and silence ruled the cabin for a spell. His mind took him back to that night six months ago, a time he had let himself revisit a lot today.

4

CATCHING COLE

Cole's First Ride Home

3/13/23

After Bill got Cole in the van and seat belted down, the van began to drive slowly toward Home. The sun was setting in the sky, and it was clear that darkness was approaching. The van was cold. It was early march in Missouri. The days could be in the seventies, or it could be freezing depending on a myriad of factors only a meteorologist could understand. For the first time Sam noticed the boy's bare legs and torso. (he still wore the spoiled shorts that he'd been wearing for many days. The smell was pretty intense, but Stan had been warned not to notice such things.)

Bill reached under the vacant passenger's seat and pulled out a blanket, opened it and handed it to Cole who wrapped himself in it like a cocoon.)

The ride only took about fifteen minutes, but the sun had long since disappeared over the horizon, and the sky was growing dark as the van pulled smoothly up to Now House.

As Bill unbuckled his seat belt, he asked Cole if he'd like some warm pajamas to wear.

The shivering boy nodded.

Bill led his new charge, who walked slightly more confidently now up the steps to the unusually large, stately looking red Brick House. They crossed the colonial looking porch past its large white pillars, and the big double doors. Without turning or speaking, Bill walked in, turned, and stopped in front of the grand staircase careful to block the view of prying eyes who might notice and peer in from the softly lit dining room. A large group of people, both kids and adults, sat consuming a family style meal at a long narrow rectangular table.

Cole let out a gasp as he entered the house. It was the biggest house he'd ever seen.

The house was truly quite grand. From its colonial columns and sprawling porches to its 8ft double front entry doors. Inside it has the appearance of a lodge with huge 14 ft ceilings on the ground floor, the floors were all coated vinyl which had the appearance of polished marble.

Every room besides the kitchen was flanked with huge, beautiful area rugs.

They entered into a grand foyer with a huge grand staircase to the right. (Just past a normal sized white door painted to match the wall. It looked miniature compared to the giant entry door) The staircase was 10 ft wide at the floor level. On the left directly across from the staircase was an open doorway trimmed in pine wood planks varnished smoothly. The doorframes on this level were all sixteen inches thick and were wrapped in pine planks. They were ten feet high and arched. Through the doorway to the left was the den.

Had the house truly been a colonial mansion, as it appeared to be, the den would have been the ballroom. It was 30 ft long and 20 ft wide. The far wall was anchored a massive light colored stone fireplace that perfectly contrasted the cherry paneled walls. The panels were 2ft wide and four feet long mounted vertically to emphasize the high ceilings. The things those walls had seen and tales they held...

The staircase gave everyone the feeling of being very small. As they made their ascent, Bill took the opportunity to remind himself that this is how all his children feel in the grown up world. At the top of the wide staircase was what seemed, to any newcomers, like a very wide hallway with rooms on both sides. From the ceiling the full width of the hall was a wood plank suspended by three links of log chain. On both sides was stenciled in dark brown against the light pine varnish the phrase "Miracles in the Making."

This phrase was on the front gate, on the porch of every house, and displayed prominently on every floor of every house.

Bill turned right and entered the first door on the Left. The room seemed small compared to the huge hallway outside. Inside were two twin beds made up, each one had a little table next to it with a small Bible its cover the same blue as the comforter on the bed. A lamp sat on each of the little tables and a cushioned straight back chair sat on the side of the table opposite the bed.

The room was also furnished with two simple looking wood chest of drawers each with a matching wooden box (for a few special toys), and a small writing desk. On the first bed made up in a plain royal blue bedspread to match the other one; was a pair of flannel pajamas, a pair of underwear folded, and a pair of thick socks. It seemed to go completely unnoticed that they all seemed to be the perfect size for their new guest.

Bill picked up the clothes and carried them back out into the hallway and into the next door on the left. It was a huge bathroom. Cole instinctively followed. The three urinals in the floor along the left wall of the room identified this as a boys' bathroom. Across from the urinals were three stalls with toilets, along a partial wall; that seemed as if it would come right out the door if it didn't stop short: leaving the perfect amount of walking room. On the back side of the partial wall were two bathtub/shower combos with thin, varnished wood sliding doors to offer protection from the potential for prying eyes. Two similar looking shower stalls lined the wall to the right of the door, while two large sinks hung on either side of the door. Bill walked Cole to the first tub on the center wall. The door was open and hanging on a towel rack on the sliding door was a big thick white towel and wash cloth. A long thin table ran down the center of the bath side of the room, with a small bench attached to it.

"Hey Cole, I'm going to put your clothes on this table in the middle." Just as I did so, I noticed that the bath had already been drawn. I checked the temperature with my hand and marveled at the intuition of my ladies. Then remembering, I spoke to Cole.

"Oh, I told you that you don't have to take a bath if you don't want to." I noticed he had slowed his pace to create distance between us, and I was immediately aware of his insecurity with taking a bath near a stranger. Once again, I had no way of knowing what horrific experiences he'd had to cause his fear, so I set about to calm them.

"I'm going to let you decide." I continued. "The special soap that our ladies make does not hurt your eyes if you get it in them, and it works for your body and your hair. I'm going to go to my sitting room across the hall. Everyone else is in the dining room eating dinner, so you may either take a bath, or just change your clothes. My name is Bill, so if you need me, you can call out and I will come. If I do not hear from you, I will call in from the door in ten minutes."

Cole just nodded, his face telling me I had eased his fears. It told me all I needed to know. It was the look of calm in the storm. I love that expression the very most. It means I anticipated the kid's fears and was able to ease them with the right words. That was a gift from God I recognize that every time. I always appreciate it when the Holy Spirit gives me the wisdom to do this.

(He made his way to the sitting room, fetched a two liter of Pepsi from the beverage refrigerator and a glass from the small hutch that sat perched in the corner. He poured a glass and sat down in the large wing backed chair at the edge of the large area rug that marked out the sitting area in the center of the room. After he took a drink, he sat the glass on the ornate side table beside his chair and took out the little leather-bound journal that he kept in the left rear pocket of his jeans.

He recounted there, in whatever detail he could recall, the little information he knew about Cole. When he finished, he slid from the chair onto his knees. There on the thick Arabian Rug, he knelt and began to pray for his new charge. He pleaded for wisdom, and for patience, and for the words to say to encourage him, and to still his fears. When he instinctively felt that about six of his ten minutes had passed, he returned to his seat, finished his soda, and then just sat quietly for the final 3-4 minutes.)

When I knocked gently on the bathroom door, I could hear the boy snoring. I gently called out,

"Cole, Cole, it's been ten minutes." If this young man was sleeping, I didn't really want to wake him, but I certainly didn't want to startle him either. My biggest fear in these situations with a new boy was that I might bring back to the surface the feelings left behind by some past trauma. You see, it's not enough to know my own intentions and motivations for the actions I take. I have to try to account for a billion untold trauma stories that could have played out in his life over his short seven or eight years.

When He didn't answer my calls, I entered the room. I was careful to make no unnecessary movements that would take moments of time during any of which the boy could awake and question my action in the light of one of those untold stories. I fetched an extra towel from the cabinet under the sink and used the towel to both cover and grab Cole. I carefully and gently reached into the now luke-warm bath water and pulled the sleeping boy out. I had one arm under his arms and one arm under his knees.

Cole seemed to stir some, but not enough to be coherent. I held the boy under his arms with one arm and gently set his feet on the tile floor. With my free arm I wrapped him in the dry towel, noticing as I did that he actually smelled like soap. He was young. I have gotten much bigger boys than this that would not have done so well under ideal conditions. These were anything but ideal conditions. Tears threatened to blur my vision as I noticed the patchwork of bruises and cuts that covered the lower half of his torso, and pretty much anything that was covered by his shorts. My heart ached with the plea, "Who could do such a thing to a little boy?"

With Cole delicately draped over my left arm by his armpits and barely perched on the tile floor, there was no way to tuck the towel into place with one arm. I just got it around him before securing it with my free arm around his knees. Thankfully, he was exceptionally light. Far too thin, and I didn't have far to go. I cradled the boy awkwardly with one arm still round his shoulders, and the other around his knees.

I learned a long time ago that a little real time ingenuity would never go unused in this work. I anticipated that the bed was on the left side of the room, where the head of the bed was, and that I'd need to lay him down with his head on the pillow at the head of the bed. With Cole draped awkwardly in my arms, I reached down and grabbed the boy's clothes. I carried the toweled boy and clothes to the bedroom.

Cole woke up enough to help me dress him and then he willingly slipped into the freshly made bed with the heavy blue comforter and the crisp white sheets. Before I reached the door of the bedroom, I could hear the boy's breathing become deep and regular. He began to snore again.

Just before leaving I tapped an inconspicuous, rectangular button exactly the same color as the cherry-stained door frame and located on the latch side exactly five feet from the floor.

This button activated an audio monitoring system that had been wired into *The Home* at construction. It would allow me to touch a single key on my phone and hear any sound in the room. I would also get an instant notification if the noise level in the room raised more than five decibels. The alert would trigger live monitoring in my phone's earpiece. It meant that if Cole called out for me, I would hear it almost immediately.

I descended the stairs quickly, but without making much noise. A task made easier by the change from my heavy boots to my crocks in the sitting room. Crocks make the best house shoes. I found the rest of my Now House charges, thirteen children (not counting Cole), having a bedtime story in the den.

Our Den was a huge room that served a multitude of purposes in Now House. It was the school Room, the entertainment room, The Chapel for daily devotions and Sunday evening Services. Tonight, it was the scene of thirteen tired faces sitting awestruck on a thick area rug in the center of the room as Stan told the Amazing Story of the Year Long Sea Voyage of Noah, His wife, their three sons, and their wives. This was usually my task, but I had to admit, Stan was doing admirably in relief. As busy as things got from time to time, I was again reminded of how blessed I am to have such an awesome team.

Stan suggested to the tired faces that after a year the eight shipmates must have begun to wonder if

God had forgotten all about them. Then He built the suspense about the return of the birds that Noah had sent out to gage if the ground was dry enough for them to emerge.

As I studied the glowing faces that beamed and shimmered with the reflection of the fire burning in the big fireplace behind Stan; I saw each of their stories play out in my mind. Impressed at how each of them had transitioned here. How sure I felt in that moment that each kid in this house desperately needed to hear the message that God is still here, even when our circumstances make us to wonder if He is.

Every one of these kids is here, because of an emergency situation that left them without safe harbor, shelter, or proper care.

While I doubted any of these kids had experienced anything remotely as traumatic as Cole; all of them have experience traumatic circumstances that would make most emblazoned, bravado, macho men cave. The only things in the adult world that compare to child trauma are rape and prisoner of war camps. How many adults come through those to be as bright and optimistic as the young men before me now, or any of the kids in the other houses. The strength of kids is truly inspiring, they truly are like plastic, durable and like Rubbermaid, they bounce back. A smile pursed my lips at the thought.

My thoughts were interrupted by an alert on my phone. I instinctively touched the earpiece with my index finger as I listened.

Cole's voice was calling out in fear.

I leapt from my chair behind the kids, crossed the fifteen feet between it and the door in two steps and took the stairs by threes. I was listening to the sounds in my ear as I reached Cole's room and entered slowly. I could hear Cole breathing. His breath was rhythmic, very heavy, and deep. I immediately knew he was sobbing.

"Cole." I waited for recognition.

The sobs stopped, and that was recognition enough. I crossed the floor, and switched on the lamp on the bedside table, careful to only switch it to the dim setting.

Cole covered his face.

I was patient, giving time to make sure he was comfortable with my presence. I also wanted him to have time to speak on his own if he chose.

(The room was quiet, as if it were filling up with the presence of the two people, the 8-year-old Cole Cupass, and the 63-year-old Bill Hinchum. Bill took a seat on the chair, and after a few minutes of silence, Cole slid his feet out from under the blankets, sat up and climbed up on Bill's lap.)

My mind was in overdrive as I willed myself not to betray my actions. I was quite surprised. I was also keenly aware that this action, though most likely innocent and if so critically important; could also be driven by some perversion from the past. Again, I reminded myself that my motives were not my only concern here. I was watching, noticing everything, while willing myself to remain calm and determined to let the situation play out until or unless a compromising action was taken.

I was surprised when Cole climbed up in my lap, but that was the purpose of the patience. I was also aware that, though the child appeared to be six or seven trauma and other developmental issues may mean he may be functioning as a much younger child right now. I didn't know enough to determine, so I observed. I wanted to give him the chance to show me what he needed.

Every kid is different, and every traumatic experience affects that child in a unique way. I was careful not to let my surprise show. I was used to the variance in responses to trauma, but I wonder if I'll ever feel prepared or worthy to deal with it.

In older boys' trauma generally drove a rather large distance between them and the world from which the trauma originated. A distance that I would have to overcome.

Affection and closeness early on are superficial especially in older kids. However, sometimes younger boys will reach for the first person they can trust as if they were falling, and instinctively know the adult is the only one who can stop the freefall. I had the distinctive impression that Cole was right then, in freefall.

Once on my lap, Cole laid his head on my Chest. His head seemed small as he lay there, and he began to sob again. After a while of just letting my arm rest on Cole's shoulders, I offered him an outlet of expression.

"Do you want to talk about it," I Asked.

"I don't like the dark" Came Cole's tiny high-pitched voice.

The remark made me instantly glad for the innovation of the night lights. One of my few suggestions to the design team. I requested that night lights be built into every bedroom in the house. Here, they were on every wall, every four feet beginning at the door of the room and four feet from the floor; a four-inch square grate on the wall which covers a small, hardwired LED light. These lights do not turn off without some real doing.

"Was it dark, Cole?" I primed again.

"They threw me away. I wasn't strong enough, and I cried too much. So, they threw me away it was so dark, I never liked the dark". Cole began emphasizing SO DARK.

(Over the next 20 minutes, Cole poured out a story that brought tears to Bill's eyes more than once. They didn't fall, but they were there. Cole's Mother was apparently a meth addict. She was always disappearing for days at a time and leaving Cole with his 10-year-old sister, Rachel.

Last week, (Bill assumed since Cole's since of time was probable off.) The two kids had run out of food, and Rachel was forced to take Cole and go looking for their mother. The search had taken them to the house on Commerce Street. Bill guessed around Tuesday.

The kids hadn't eaten anything in 3 days and were starting to have bad hunger pains. They went to Commerce Street to try to find their mother but interrupted a party. They were told she was in the bedroom. When the kids went in there Rachel was told to put Cole in the Closet.

From the dark closet Cole heard his sister repeated screams and cries. Cole explained that he heard many grown-ups come into the room and hurt Rachel, and then she was taken away. He told Bill that Rachel tried to fight, but they were too big.)

"She said no," shaking his head, "but nobody listened they wanted her to do terrible yucky things and they hurt her." He went on to say that he heard other people screaming and crying too. When he tried to come out to help her, a man hit him three or four times, and slammed the closet door in his face.

(Cole just laid down and covered his ears until the police found him. He explained that he doesn't know where his sister or his mama could be.)

"When I sleep, I can hear the screaming and crying. I can feel the darkness of the closet. I feel like I might never get..." Cole's sobs overtook him.

I've learned to be very patient when little ones begin to talk. It's hard for them to get the courage, and it sometimes takes time for them to find the words to use. I've also learned that sometime what they don't say tells as much as what they do.

Cole didn't say anything that explained the cuts and bruises Bill had seen, and he didn't explain what he wasn't strong enough for, or what it was that made him cry, or even why they threw him away. He also didn't explain how he knew they were asking Rachel to do "terrible, yucky things"

Bill didn't consider these inconsistencies as an honestly issue, but rather as a communication or a trust issue. He either doesn't know the answers from the holes Bill was noticing, or he didn't trust him enough to say. Bill knew from the child's injuries and from the injuries he'd seen that there was a great deal more to this trauma than had been contained in this first telling.

He could easily know that things were painful, because of her cries, but he couldn't know how yucky something was unless he witnessed or experienced it.

I patted Cole's shoulders and reassured him that it wasn't his fault. I told him how brave a boy he was. "The men were very big. Only a very strong, brave boy could have kept his cool and protected yourself by staying in the closet."

After Cole told his story, we just sat there for a long time. I wanted to give Cole time for anything else to come to the surface that he might want to share.

When I was relatively sure that Cole was not going to share any more right now, I got an idea. I would try to get him to the kitchen for some sleepy time tea. That might help him sleep, and I had a pretty popular recipe. I asked Cole if he would like to try a really yummy drink that might help him go back to sleep.

Cole nodded.

Over the next several days Cole revealed that He actually had not spent all that time in the closet. The truth was much more sinister. He and Rachel had walked into a party that included some very young guests who had not come willingly. They had been purchased for a block of time. The time expired before the appetite did Cole and Rachel arrive shortly after these sick games had been forced to end. They picked up where they'd left off with their hired boys, however these two were far too weak to withstand the physical strain of what they wanted.

Cole lost consciousness in the closet after being used for hours until he grew too weak to meet their demands and was cast away in the closet, presumed dead or dying.

Bill remembered thinking Overdosing on meth was far too easy a death for those who would do such things to children. He must always guard himself against such thoughts, not wanting to dwell either on the horrors that were imposed on the victims or those he might deem appropriate for those who inflicted them.

Now, perhaps you see why Bill would be forced to fight back tears of joy when he looked at the vibrant, boy with the dancing eyes and chirpy voice. He wonders if that's how God feels when he sees the great redwoods. We see the magnificence of what's above the ground, how much more majestic and impressive it must be for one who understands how much of that strength and magnificence come from the struggle that takes place below the surface. It's sort of like that with kids. Everyone else sees what and how they are now. We compare them one to another never stopping to consider the invisible struggle that so few will ever see.

Its why Bill's eyes filled with tears when he saw Cole leap into the dumpster today to help Jeff. He seemed not to hesitate, but Cole still has real struggles with confinement and darkness. Both of those factors were potentially present in the dumpster. However, he leapt right in. It's pretty impressive.

5

MIGHTY MEN

Today

5:27 PM

As the van pulled up to the huge house, Bill heard the sound of which he would never tire, awe.

"Are we stopping here!?" Jeff asked his excitement peeking through in the crescendo and spiking tone in his voice which came completely unabated just now.

Bill had to admit he felt it too. Every time he drove through the front gates. As he parked the van, he shot Debra a quick text... "New Boy, I'll clean face. Cole's size"

"Cole, would you please show Jeff up to your room, help him find some dry clothes, then bring him to meet me in the den? Bill asked, careful not to sound too commanding.

"Sure Dad" the words warmed Bill's heart even if they did sound pretty awkward. That was the first real acknowledgement Cole had made about the proceedings earlier today.

Bill had actually wondered what he was feeling about it. That was his answer. As the boys disappeared into the house, Bill dialed Chief.

"David, Any missing kids?"

"Nope," came the chief's response.

"I'm not surprised. He was assaulted by his stepdad and stepped in to help his mom. I'll give you more on injuries after I clean him up.

"How's Jack?" the chief asked.

"Amazing! He's going to take over for me. He jumped into a dumpster today and came out with a kid!"

"I think you're right! Not even been yours for a day, and already saving kids. I thought he didn't like small spaces?"

"He doesn't Dave, that's the thing, but as soon as he heard there was a kid in there it's like he came to life! I'm telling you this kid was terrified of me. It was all Cole! He jumped in there, talked to him for a couple minutes, then led him out. It was amazing!" Bill made no attempt to squelch the mix of pride, excitement, and praise dripping from his voice.

"Well congratulations! Now you know what I've been watching for the last 10 years! He ain't even been yours an hour, and already a chip off the old block!" That is something. That's for sure! That is something! Hey, I'm going to call over to the hospitals and see if they've had any women come in that could be a DV. Maybe we can find his mom." said the chief.

"Sounds good. I'll get in here and get him cleaned up and see what we can learn. Thanks chief, see ya soon."

"Hey Bill, I think I'm going take off tomorrow. "You don't need me. You don't just break 'em. Now you're rounding 'em up too. Think I'll just take a vacation day."

"Better not chief, by tomorrow this thread's going unravel a whole new crime syndicate for you to take down. You'll be head of the FBI by next week. "

"Yeah, I'll be waiting for your call Mr. President."

Bill entered the house to the sound of a grand sword fight in the den. The wooden swords were clanging, and the spectators were cheering. Tom and Aiden were going at it. They had obviously been studying, because both boys had their free hands tucked behind their backs and were exhibition form the likes of which hadn't been seen since the invention of the handgun.

Bill immediately went into something akin to coach mode. He began giving pointers and coaching both boys. Eventually Tom was fatally wounded and gave a great show of collapsing in a bloody heap on the floor. Bill immediately stood pretending to be annoyed, demanding what was the meaning of this, and why they had allowed a murder to take place on his rug.

Stan appeared, taking full responsibility, and vowing to have any bloodstained promptly removed. Everyone laughed, and just like that, Stan retook the room and continued a spirited rendition of a story staring David and his mighty men retaking their wives and children who had all been taken by the enemy. He concluded that it was true, and that some very terrible things were in store for these women and children had they been left in the hands of the enemy. However, God had not abandoned them to the whims of the enemy, but had sent a rescue. When there was nothing, they could do for themselves, God sent a rescue.

Bill was leaning against the doorframe with his back to the staircase when he heard the sound behind him. He turned slowly to see Jeff and Cole sitting on the stairs. Both boys seemed to be emotional. Cole had storm clouds on his face, but Jeff was crying outright.

I stepped across the hall and sat down between the two boys on the bottom step. "Now what is happening here," I asked in a low voice focused first on Jeff. The pastor in me suspecting this was more spiritual than emotional.

"Is it really true, does God really rescue moms and kids from getting hurt? Cause I been wishin', and hopin', and dreamin' of someone to help me and my mom for a long, long time now. People shouldn't hurt people. They shouldn't try to make 'em scared and feel small. We need some mighty men like in the story. I just never met anyone like that before." Jeff sniffed.

"You're right Jeff, we sure do need more mighty men who will be kind and loving, and who will protect ladies and children. That's how God planned it, that men would be that way. You know what Jeff, there are some men like that, and you're going meet some. My friend David is going to come to talk to you later today or in the morning. I think he's one of those men." I was careful to keep my voice slow and low not wanting to rush him.

"Are you one of those men?" Jeff asked, looking up at me.

"I sure hope so, son, I hope so." I immediately regretted using the word son. I was usually careful not to use it with kids that hadn't been adopted yet, careful not to give false hope.

When I looked over at Cole tears were streaming down his face now.

"Yes, you are, Dad, yes you are. You are a mighty man. You rescued all of us." He was sobbing now. It was partly deep conviction that was choking the boy up.

I put my arm around his shoulders. He leaned the side of his head against me and hugged me tight. I returned his hug.

"I wanna be a mighty man too. I wanna rescue people, Bill. Do you think I could?" his voice almost pleading now.

"Well son, I think from what I saw today you most certainly can. I'd even say you were a might man today. What do you think, Jeff? Would you have been able to trust me today if it weren't for Cole?" Turning back to the new boy.

"No sir, I was pretty scared." Jeff answered honestly.

There was one mighty man out their today. I was just his driver, I said turning to Cole and ruffling his hair. "Now," I stood and turned to face both boys, "How about we see to the cuts on you face and head Jeff? Cole, would you like to give us a hand?"

We cleaned up Jeff's face and head, and reported to Chief on his injuries, when given the choice Jeff decided to stay.

6

NEW BEGINNINGS

3/14/23

In The Morning on the Coffee Porch with a full pot of steaming coffee, a cup in his hand, a journal, a Bible, a pen, and the rolling green hills of Home…His day was beginning in the absolute perfect way.

(The only improvement would be a lovely lady to share it all with, but that dream had long since been given to The Dream Keeper.)

He's already read three chapters from his Bible and taken a good ten pages of notes in the little journal. Thoughts on the scriptures, and a record of an honest conversation with his dearest and most cherished friend.

His eyes wandered down the short path to "And Ever House." It was here that he generally made his home with his six young kids that looked to him to lead in evening prayers, and offer the morning devotion, comfort, and guide them into the abyss of adulthood. He was "Dad to every one of them by this point." His kids, have all been with him for some time at Now, and through the adoption process that included the transition into And Ever House.

Eventually the circumstances of their lives had reached the point where they could no longer safely return to their previous homes or to a placement with blood relatives. For each one a time came when a new forever home was needed.

At that point, careful to ensure that the fit in the house was something he felt he could manage, Bill would call them out to this very spot. This little coffee porch, as he called it. It was a small gazebo outside Now house, about halfway down the little path that led to And Ever House. It sat atop one of the small gentle hills that made up the property. Sort of his own little command tower...The coffee porch overlooked the entire place but had been purposely constructed with a direct path to each House.

Bill hoped that every child that he ushered through the front gates would eventually sit with him in this special place where the breeze blows gently, the water streamed in the little garden pond, and the birds sing beautifully all day long, or so it seemed. It was one little corner of this horrible, twisted world that just seemed right.

He knew it was selfish to think this way, wanting to keep every kid; but he did all the same. Of course, the rhetoric was that we always hope that biological parents could get their stuff together and be able to make a reasonably safe place where they could and would properly care for their children. It wasn't even that this wasn't a huge part of the story of Now House. It was, but that was part of Bill's way. He had to feel that he was the only hope, and no one else was going to help. It's what made him push with every kid to get through, to make a difference, to never take even one life for granted.

Plus, after he was aware of the parental and familiar breakdowns that facilitated the level of abuse and neglect that these children had endured, secretly he had an extremely tough time having any reasonable expectation that the safety nets would provide any more protection in the future than they had in the past.

He recalled the definition of "insanity" that so many used in this work...doing the same thing over and over, expecting a different result. So many times, that is exactly what had been done with these kids. Authorities gave the same warnings, took the same steps, placed these kids (or left them) in the same dangerous environments; then expect the same neglectful, abusive, or outright predatory adults not to allow or cause these kids to be hurt again.

Sometimes, he acknowledged, the medicine can be worse than the sickness too. The desperation of authorities to remove children from moderately dangerous environments, can cause them to rush to recruit and license, and then maintain a blind spot where certain homes are concerned. This leading them to continue to place and keep kids in out of home care that might do as much or more damage than if they'd just left those kids alone at home.

"Don't get me wrong," He'd written long ago in his journal, "I believed in giving individuals second chances all you want. I just don't believe you can, in good conscience, do that by putting another's life in the balance!" It was one of the rare subjects that could ignition the inner passions and arouse the fervent anger of this typically very temperate man.

His eyes drifted to And Ever House and his thoughts followed. He whispered a prayer of gratitude for Sandy and Debora. He imagined them now rousing his little princes from their beds and ushering them in for Breakfast. He truly had the best team that he could have ever dreamed of. He certainly had the right Human Resources team! "Those two have been with me since we only had the one house, and we just kept packing little charges into that house, and then there was Jenifer. …"

His focus was broken this morning by the vibration of his phone. Curious, he pulled it from his pocket. It was Mark texting him. Mark, a sixteen-year-old adopted son, and resident of And Ever House would usually never text this early.

I immediately hit the call button. "Hey Son, what's up."

"Hey dad, I'm sorry to bother you."

"Woe. Stop right there for a second. You could not bother me I love you, what's up?"

"I don't know dad. It's just a bunch of stuff. ACTs on Saturday I have a huge Math test that whipping my tail…" Mark began.

"Hey, enough said. Wrap up whatever you've got going and come to the porch. Bring your bag, stop at the kitchen, and ask Sandy to bring our breakfast out here. I'll drive you to school if necessary. We can steal back the time you would have spent on the bus. You don't ever hesitate to call me son. I will always have time for you."

"Ok. I just need a little time to finish this math assignment. Thanks. I'll see ya in a minute." Mark said.

Bill whispered a prayer for Mark. Soon his thoughts returned to Jennifer)

Jennifer had come to us when John was about to become a fixture. The Local DFS supervisor had concluded that the only solution was to separate those two. Jen, as her nick name would come to be, would become a real Gem, but John had just been in too much trouble. He had been asked to leave several foster homes for behavioral reasons. Well, let's be honest now, that's not exactly how those conversations go. He'd come home from school and see the worker's car in the drive. "I've come to take you to your new placement," she'd say. Or the first time he questioned the foster parent (his questioning could be rather forceful), or my favorite, the first spat with the biological son who was also his new roommate. (That spat was over whether John should perform "special favors" in exchange for staying in his room.)

It didn't seem surprising at all to Bill, that John was angry after being passed back and forth as the punching bag and personal plaything of an unusually cruel and twisted uncle and stepdad. He was full of anger and struggling to find any form of expression that was not abusive or disruptive.

"He is nowhere near the challenge that he was when he came to us," bill thought, "but to pretend all that trauma and the struggles that come with it would just be washed away by a bit of time and new examples would not be even close to honest."

Bill understood all too well that John's trauma would be with him all his life, but "So long as he acknowledges it, sets the right standards for his own behavior, and keeps his focus on Christ; he will live to overcome it rather than having it overcome him." Bill had told John this on his 16th birthday The outside of the card read, "To My Son" on the front. Inside he had penned a long note that he hoped would one day take root in his son's heart.

Jennifer saw how well John was adjusting to being home and how much he missed her, so she asked Bill if it would be possible for her to come too. Bill thought long and hard about that before making that decision. Bringing a teenage girl into a house of boys was pretty risky, and potentially unwise.

Bill eventually gave in to the idea. He already had two adult, but young women who lived on the third floor of the house. When he shared his dilemma with them, it was immediately settled. They had a large study that they never used. They did all their studying in the sitting room anyway. Bill would have had a mutiny on his hands had he tried to say no.

A smile crossed his lips now, as he thought about the three women and how wonderful a decision it had been.

His eyes fell back over the two little hills to rest on Forever House. It had been his home for so long.

Just then, his thoughts were interrupted again by his phone. He actually was seldom bothered during his time of solitude here. He glanced down to see a text from Tad.

"Hey Pops, I'm flying in with dad this morning to check out my new houses. If you're not busy, I'd like to see you. Dad has work in Springfield, but I think I'm going to grab a rental and come on down. Maybe… ten-ish…?"

Bill smiled as he sent his response. He hadn't seen Tad in six and a half months. He was busy serving as an assistant youth pastor in the church his grandfather used to pastor. He felt a hint of excitement add a few beats-per-minute to his heart.

It would take something pretty drastic to miss the chance to see Tad. He was such a huge part of all this. Even before Forever House there was Tad.

At first, he had dreamed so small, fearing even to apply to be a foster parent. With just a two-bedroom apartment and being single; it just seemed so far-fetched. Then he just did it, finally made the call. He smiled again as he thought of how everything cascaded from that first call….

Susie Whirl had returned his call. It was August 2018, and she was about to begin her first experience teaching the Foster Parent Class.

She would later share with Bill how she had tried to quit after the loss of the child that she had recommended be returned to his biological parents. Six weeks. That's how long it took for the boy's stepdad to beat the 8-year-old half to death before strangling him.

"The shock almost turned away one of the real gems of the child welfare system," Bill thought. He remembered how excited and nervous he was when he graduated from his training. It was a bigger accomplishment since only half the class finished training. Two other couples and Bill. Thinking about this, now, lead Bill to stand and take the two steps to cross his porch to open the nearly unseen hinged door at the end of a small built-in cabinet in one corner. Inside, well insulated from the elements, were three shelves of small leather journals and other notebooks. He reached in and took the one from the very far left.

Back in his chair he opened the little leather-bound notebook titled, "Something New" and began to relive the very beginning. As he scanned his own words the events streamed back to his mind like it was happening all over again….

He was living in a little two-bedroom apartment on the edge of town. He was about a year and half out from watching his marriage fall apart, ending his pastoral career. His family and ministry had been his life, and he was devastated. It took him that first year to finally start to emerge from the cloud of depression that threatened to completely claim him.

He had finally realized he had surrendered his life to the adversary for an entire year and was unwilling to give up another moment. He had grown up in foster care and had always wanted to get involved.

After making it through Susie's class, he was excited about the adoption event. It was going to be a catered dinner, but the highlight was that there would be fifteen kids that were available for adoption. They would be there, and the newly licensed adoptive parents would meet them. If they hit it off, they would begin the paperwork to take them home.

Bill was sure that with his own two kids coming over every other weekend, this whole adoption thing would be complicated. He had stayed up all night praying the night before the event, and he had a plan.

Bill showed up at the Community Church on Friday afternoon, January 24, 2020. He was two hours early and waited fifteen minutes until he saw Susie go in. He hurried up to the door and followed. He had to ask her a question.

When he entered the building, Susie was on the phone, and he waited patiently, giving her plenty of room to preserve her privacy.

"Bill, you know that you are very early, don't you?" She asked as she hung up her phone.

"Y y yes," he stammered, nervous now. "I thought you might need some help setting up." It was half lie and half ice breaker.

"Well, I think I've got it covered. How are you feeling about today?" Susie bailed him out.

"Well, I did want to talk to you before anybody gets here. I need you to point out to me the kid that has experienced the most trauma." Bill explained hesitantly.

Susie's face began to cloud with a puzzled expression. She was used to new foster and especially adoptive parents seeking the least traumatized, best adjusted children to bring into their home.

Bill saw the question in her expression and continued without needing to be asked. "Susie, if you were a lifeguard standing on the side of a pool and saw two kids struggling in the water at the same time. One child is a 10-year-old in the 3ft (who just needs to stand up) and the other is a 3-year-old in the 12 ft. Which one would you save?"

"Sure the 10-year-old could drown in three feet of water, easily. But anyone can tell him to stand up, and it is very likely that somebody will. If I don't get to that 3-year-old, he is going to die. I've waited to do this my whole life. And, depending on how this goes, I might not ever do it again. I need to make the greatest impact possible. I know it's unusual, but I need your help." He hoped his had successfully communicated this thought.

Susie looked at Bill for several minutes before she answered. She later explained that at that moment she was forced to step over all of her past experience and training. What she did next would transform hundreds of lives, not the last of which was Bill Hinchum's.

Finally, she shrugged. "Ok Bill, then go over to my office. A foster mother is about to drop off Tad Johnson. He's fifteen. He's just been in another fight at school. Four kids are injured and three are headed to the hospital. They cannot keep him anymore because he's been expelled from school. I'm going to have to move him to residential treatment. Again, if I can't find him a placement today." The emphasis she placed on this was not really offered for Bill's sake, but just came from her deep concern. "And, there aren't any more programs available that I would choose."

"Talk to him," she continued. "Get acquainted with him. If you think it's too much, come back over here, and look at these kids. If not, I'll leave word with Ginger Massey to start the paperwork. Right now, he's just a foster. I know you're looking to adopt, but he's just a foster. It is possible, things could develop a bit more, but as of now.... I will have his file waiting for you."

"...And, Bill," she was shaking her head for emphasis. "I hope you know what you're asking for, because all the kids we're going to have over here are in the shallow end of the pool."

At the office Bill went to the desk and asked for Ginger Massey. Ginger was a very well dressed, middle-aged woman, a little short, and stalky. Her face was round, and her hair was just starting to turn from brown to gray. Bill thought it odd that she didn't die it.

Ginger started to show Bill to the room where Tad was waiting, but before she could open the door with the one-foot square window in the center: Bill stopped her. Placing his hand innocently on the inside of her elbow as he followed.

"I thought I would get to see his file first?" he asked.

"Sorry," she began, "I haven't had a chance to pull it yet. Go ahead and visit him, and I'll pull it and have it for you in a little while.

Bill entered the room where Tad, a tall thin young man with the red hair to match the temper Bill had heard about. Apparently, the incident at school, happened in Gym, because Tad was still dressed out in a white tank top and blue sweats. His arms and shoulders carried some definition, but he didn't strike Bill as one who would inflict the degree of damage that had been reported.

"Hi, I'm Bill."

"Uh, why am I talking to you? I'm waiting for Susie." Tad protested. His voice carried a mix of dismissiveness and defiance. He raised and deepened his voice for affect and seemed to puff himself up in the shoulders.

Bill acted as if he hadn't noticed the boy's posturing reaction to his presence. It did not seem unusual or unexpected to him. He remembered noticing, but dismissing the thought almost as quickly as its recognition appeared. It was a trauma reaction that Bill had known well, like an old friend that you notice in the corner of photo. "Tad, I'll make a deal with you. I will shoot straight with you if you'll shoot straight with me." Bill said, about to see how out-matched he really was.

"Ok" Tad answerer, his expression saying "ok, I'll play along."

"Tad, I've not had a conversation with a foster kid in 20 years. I understand that you got into some trouble today. Susie's in a meeting right now, but when she gets over here, she's going to start looking for a residential treatment facility to take you. I understand this won't be the first time?"

"Actually Tad, I'm a new foster parent. I showed up early to an adoption event earlier, I heard you were over here and that you might have to go to residential treatment. I figured I have some time to kill, so I came over to visit."

"What's an adoption event?" Tad interrupted, His voice raising now. His face held an inquisitive look.

Bill barely noticed the way He was able to slice through everything Bill said to pull out the one piece of information that he wanted to discuss. This would become a skill, perhaps a trauma-power that Bill would have to learn to navigate in the months and years ahead.

"It's a show and tell for social workers to show off kids that are ready for an adoptive family. Some of those kids might go home with a real shot at a forever home." Bill said knowing all too well how important that dream was to anybody in foster care as long as Tad.

"How come I ain't never been to one of those things? I didn't even know they existed." Tad inquired, anger tinging his voice.

"Well Tad, it's like I said. They are for kids that are ready for a forever family. It seems to me that your behavior seems to say you're not." Bill said in a level tone.

Tad's face began turning a dark red as his jaw clinched. He said nothing, but he looked away.

Bill remembered waiting for Tad to explode at him, sensing that the subject had touched a very raw nerve in him. However, it seemed like the silence served as a pressure valve draining off the extra pressure until Tad could answer reasonably.

"I don't know what to do about that. People just make me mad. ...all the time." Tad said a defeated look coming over his face.

Bill wondered if this was the first sign of Tad's armor cracking, but assured himself it was far too early for that. (From his perspective on the coffee porch this morning, He knew that's exactly what it was.)

Just then, Ginger opened the door and handed Bill a file about two and a half inches thick with Tad Johnson's name on it.

Bill held it in his hand for a moment before looking at Tad. Thinking....

Ginger closed the door behind her as she left.

"How long have you been in the system, Tad." Bill asked.

"Since I was five why?" Tad asked, his defensiveness going virtually unnoticed by Bill.

Bill thought for a moment before tossing the file on the table in front of Tad. "Do you think that file has every piece of paper that's been written on you in 10 years?" Bill asked, not hiding the disdain in his own voice.

"No way! That wouldn't even hold the write up of all the times I been in trouble at school! They never give new foster parents much. They're afraid. If you had any idea what you're getting into, you'd run, run like the wind." Tad's voice was light, but Bill noticed a hint of a softer, somber tone too.

"Tad, if I could help you with your temper, and try to get you to a point where you could be ready for a forever family, would you help me figure out this whole foster parent thing?"

Several minutes passed, before Tad answered in a creaky softer voice blending into sarcasm but without the combative element to his tone that he'd used before. "I would, but they'll never let a newbie have me. I'm too bad. They already said I will never have a real family."

"Let me worry about that for a bit, Tad" Bill answered in a light, optimistic tone. "I'll be right back."

Bill walked out the door to the desk and asked Ginger to bring him the paperwork. Ginger appeared behind the receptionist with a panicked look on her face.

"Um, Ok, I'll...I'll get them right out to you." Ginger said hurriedly.

Bill walked back to the interview room, and asked Tad what kind of soda he liked.

"Root beer." Tad answered.

Bill set out to find a soda machine. He returned with a Root beer for Tad and Pepsi for himself. As he sat back down, he gestured to the file he'd left lying on the table. He handed the root beer to Tad, and asked, "so how much is in it?"

At first Tad tried to act like he *didn't* touch the folder or look inside.

Bill raised an eyebrow. "Oh, it's changed that much in 24 years? Now they talk to kids, so you don't need to look what they're saying about you when someone leaves your file laying around?" His voice was dripping with sarcasm.

Tad blushed a little and looked like he'd been caught with his hand in the cookie jar. "Ok, I may have taken a quick peek."

"A quick peek? I saw you drop it when I came back to ask what kind of soda, then I was gone 10 minutes searching for them. Level with me. How far off are they?" Bill said in a firm, but playful tone.

"Well," Tad began, "They mostly left out the stuff I didn't do anyways." His lips curled in a rye smile, realizing he couldn't fool Bill.

"Oh, they did, did they? That's awfully convenient. Not today, but soon we're going to have to talk about your honesty." Bill said with a playful grin.

7

GREATEST NEEDS

Tad rolled his eyes, but he was grinning. Just then the door opened with the papers for Bill to sign.

Bill accepted them, and as he began to flip through, scanning each page. He stopped and looked up at Tad. "If I sign this, I am taking responsibility for your safety, and the safety of others as a result of your actions." His gaze was not focused on anything as he considered the decision, sure to let his words hang in the air to soak in. He wanted Tad to know that he was taking some risk, even if it was pretty undefined. He let the words hang and fade into silence for a few minutes before setting the stack of papers back on the table and returned his focus back to Tad.

"Tad I'm in this for keeps. I just told Susie this morning that I don't know if I'm ever going to do this again. I'm in this process with the hopes of adopting someone out of this mess. I know you have no reason to believe me, but if I sign these papers, I'm making the decision to stay with you and keep fighting for you forever. Even if they don't ever let me adopt you. Even if they decide that I can't keep you." He paused again.

"Tad how did you get here?"

Tad attempted to hand Bill the file off the table, but Bill did not accept it.

"I don't want to know what the file says. I want to know what you say." As these words hung in the air, Bill noticed something. Tad's expression changed and he actually looked younger to him. Not a little either. It was significant. His shoulders slumped; his face softened. The vibrato seemed to drain from his whole demeanor and offer a glimpse at the terrified and broken little boy that he really was. Bill would one day come to call this when the armor comes off or the shell cracks. He'd seen a crack earlier, but it seemed to disappear as quickly as it appeared. This was something else.

"I dunno," Tad said. "I guess my parents couldn't take care of me." Tad said his tone becoming slightly dismissive as his voice trailed off. He was trying to regain his toughness, to restore his armor; but it was a half-hearted effort that only lasted a few seconds. It reminded Bill of a car trying to turn over with a dead battery.

"Ok." Bill said, that's what you've been told by other people, but those people aren't you? This is your life. I want to know what you remember; what you know about how you got here."

"I don't know I was little. I just know I've been in a lot of different families, and nobody wants me. I get in trouble, and they throw me back. Its just how things work." Tad said, his tone raised, but tears formed in his eyes.

"It seems like you're pretty angry. Where does that come from?" Bill asked.

"I don't know," Tad's expression dropped more (Bill thought he would cry)" I just get mad. I think about my parents. Why don't they want me? Every home I go to. Why do they never want me? I know I'm bad, but other kids do bad stuff too. People still love them."

Bill could remember the feelings that Tad was describing. They were raw, burning in his own chest as Tad spoke.

"You know that if you go to residential treatment, you will probably be with older boys. A lot of stuff happens in those places that's not part of the treatment. I spent some time in a place like that once." Bill said, barely aware that he was thinking out loud. He was struggling to know the right thing to do. He wanted to sign the papers, but what if Tad really needed treatment? But the last thing that Tad said seemed to play on repeat in his heart and mind.

"Other people do bad stuff. people still love them." That was it. He realized that what Tad was desperate for was the one thing he couldn't get in residential treatment. Tad needs love. That's the one thing everyone had been forbidden to give him as a foster kid.

Distance, Distance, Distance. That's what he kept hearing all through his training. His own heart had ached every time he heard it. That's exactly what these kids have had ever since they came into the system. What they longed for, he knew, was closeness. They needed love, and here in front of him was a boy with 10 years of behavior history, and Bill felt that all of it was this little boy's desperate plea for love. It's his reaction to being denied that basic human need.

He did not miss it when Tad Said, "I know." To his statements about residential and he could hear the knowing in the boy's tone.

Bill picked up the stack of papers and pulled the pen from his shirt pocket and began quickly to search out the colored sticky arrows identifying the signature lines. Then halfway through the packet, he stopped. He had forgotten that he had decided if he did sign these papers, he would ask Tad first.

"Tad, I already started these, but I'll tear them up if you don't want me to sign them. Do you want me to do this? Like I said, I'm not a hotel. I'm signing this to be your family, not your babysitter. At times not your friend, I'm not promising to do what you want, but I'm committing to do what I think you need. If that's something, you really want."

Tad nodded, but his face was full of emotion. Bill thought it looked like a sky that was clouding up before a thunderstorm.

Bill felt the emotion in his own chest. What he had decided to do for Tad today, no one had ever done for him. He wanted to hug Tad, but he figured there would be time for that when both of them were more comfortable.

Tad's voice was soft as he spoke now. "So, you're saying that you want to be my family? You want to fight for me? You want to keep me forever? Even though I'm bad?" His voice trailed off, but he was not finished.

"You know I got in a fight today. I hurt people. It's not the first time either." He hesitated with each question and statement as if laying them out in the air for Bill to inspect.

"Yes Tad. You know how this works. Case workers and judges make the decisions, but I want to be your family. I want to be with you forever. Everyone is bad sometimes. We all mess up. We still need love. Tad, I waited my whole life to hear someone say that. I know what it's like to wait for it, to long for it.

It's hard, and it hurts, not a little. I'm in it now. I know that it will take you awhile to really understand that, but I'm in…all the way in."

Tad's face revealed what Bill knew. He was hopeful but hesitant, cautiously optimistic. Bill knew it would take time for this to be real to Tad.

Today

10/14/23 -

Bill wiped the tears from his eyes as he took a drink of his cold coffee on the coffee porch. Tad had unlocked something deep inside him. He forced Bill to revisit and reprocess all of his own feelings of abandonment. Tad would challenge Bill's commitment over the next year or so until one day he just accepted that Bill would not send him away.

…It was September of 2020, now. Tad had been with Bill about 9 months and the two had discussed the fact that Bill believed he was being led by the Lord to take in more boys. The conversation happened over Pizza on a Friday night. Tad said yes, but after the two had retired for the night, he became conflicted. He was convinced that Bill would choose the new kids over him and send him away. He had been rejected enough that it always seemed like the more natural outcome than Bill remaining committed.

Tad rose early on Saturday and took a kitchen knife and slit all four tires on their Ford Explorer.

Bill was more confused and hurt than angry. He thought Tad would like to do for other boys, what Bill had done for him. He knew that Tad was all too accustomed to the pain of abandonment and rejection. Bill called for Tad, and he was met at the door of their apartment; Tad's bags were already packed.

"I guess I'll be going to residential now." Tad announced, "only we're going to need a ride."

Bill remembered he didn't say a word. He walked past Tad to his little office in the corner of his own bedroom. He opened his laptop and typed out a contract in which he swore to never send Tad away no matter what negative behavior he ever did. He even said that the contract was good until his death. He called a friend who drove the two to the bank where he had the signature on the document notarized.

(They would eventually frame this document and hang it in Tad's bedroom, so whenever he started thinking that Bill would abandon him, he could remind himself of the commitment that his caretaker had made.) Tad found Bill on the patio later that day and hugged him with tears streaming down his face. He apologized for the tires and promised never to do anything like that ever again.

"I know;" Bill told him, hugging him. "You are just going to have to accept that I love you."

"I love you too, Dad." Tad responded. That was the first time he ever called Bill Dad. It was a very pivotal moment in their relationship.

About Six weeks later In November, they sat in church with Bill's two biological sons Moses James and Noah Allen. Tad began to cry, before getting up from his seat, mid-message and heading out the back door. Bill followed. Tad crumpled on the floor in the small foyer, sobbing.

Bill gave him as much space as he could in the small room and didn't speak for a few moments, sensing that someone was already talking that he wasn't meant to hear at the moment.

Tad felt his presence and asked, "Can God love somebody like me?"

Bill let the question linger in the air before answering. "Well, he loved Saul of Tarsus. He was a murderer. He said He loves all. Do you think that includes you?"

"Yes, but how do you feel that? I don't know how to feel that." Tad said in a desperate tone.

"Tad, do you think I love you?" Bill asked quietly.

"Yes." Tad looked up through his tears.

"But there are times you don't feel that." Bill suggested.

"I guess so." Tad answered.

"The sun does not disappear at night or when it's cloudy outside. You can't see it, but you can know that it's still there." Bill explained. "If we can feel God's love or not doesn't have anything to do with weather its real. We know that God never lies. He tells us that he loves all and gave himself to die for the sins of all. He wants to forgive us for those sins and make us clean and adopt us into his family forever." Bill explained, feeling he knew where this exchange was headed, and praying he was right.

"Dad, I know he loves me, even if I don't understand why. I know I have a lot of sin. More than most kids. I want to be part of his family. I'm just not sure how to do it." Tad explained.

Well Tad. Even though God has done everything that needed to be done for you to be forgiven and adopted into His family, He will not force you. He is a gentleman. He offers this to you. He waits patiently for you to decide that you want it and ask for it. You just have to be ready to leave your sin behind." Bill told him.

"I want to do that dad. I want to ask him. Will you help me?" Tad asked.

Today

3/14/23-

It was a remarkable story Bill acknowledged as he freshened up his coffee. If that were the end of the story it would have accomplished more than Bill could ever have imagined, but it was not the end. Two weeks later Tad was baptized after a special Thanksgiving Service in the church they attended. Bill wrote a social media post highlighting Tad's story. He was careful not to identify Tad by name so as to avoid breaching his confidentiality.

That post grabbed the attention of an old friend of Bill's, a writer for a large Christian newspaper. He wanted to do a full write up on Tad. Bill and Tad had dinner with Tom Crusland. He asked a lot of questions, and they departed the restaurant expecting that what they had shared would be edited and tweaked and would appear in the story.

However, Tom was a bit of an investigative journalist. He did some digging. A couple months later on January 10th, Bill received an email from Tom. He attached all of his research for the article and explained that he felt it was not a good time to send it to print. He urged Bill to review his notes and get back to him with any questions.

Bill was surprised, but his curiosity led him to click the link. Tom had managed to discover and include some details about the circumstances around which Tad had been taken into custody, that if it was anywhere in the records Bill had never seen it.

The article told what they knew …that Tad's mother, Barbara Johnson, was involved with illegal drug activity and was known to sell "personal" services in exchange for money or drugs. (Those services often extended to her little boy—this wasn't in the article) Tad Johnson was picked up in a drug raid. He was found locked in his bedroom without anything to eat or drink. His Mother's parental rights had been terminated due to a persistent inability to gain stability and stay out of police custody.

What they didn't know, was that Tom had discovered Tad Johnson was the result of a very brief relationship with one Johnny Timmons. That wouldn't mean too much, unless you were up to speed on the tech scene or followed business.

(Johnny Timmons was the founder of *Screenwhip*. *Screenwhip* was an innovative app released in 2012 and rediscovered in May of 2020 during the Coronavirus Pandemic when the country was shut down.

The app managed to integrate with any virtual meeting app, document generating, videography, and slideshow apps. It allowed the user to whip the screen of any meeting attendee onto the monitors of everyone in attendance in real time by hitting a single keystroke. It was innovative, efficient, and had been updated to work on every platform with every app. The timing was perfect as everyone was trying to figure out how to make virtual business faster, simpler, and easier. It was a slam dunk in terms of ease of use. The once unknown company literally went viral overnight, and Timmons sold the app to Google for 247 million in August of 2020.

Timmons' relationship with Johnson was when he was still in college back in 2002, and apparently the two had not been in contact since.

Wow! Bill remembered how shocked he had been. He called Tom immediately to inquire about his source. Which he shared freely. He had spoken to Barbara Johnson in the Green County Jail.

"Bill," Tom told him, "she says he knew about the boy and wanted to see him, but she ran away.

That's why I killed the story. You guys decide what you want to do about it. Tad was born in Kansas City to Barbara Johnson, but She changed her name two weeks before the baby was born. Her given name was Carry Collins, and she was a schoolmate of Timmons. Two weeks after the child was born, she left the Kansas City area and says she's never been back. Her family is all in Kansas, so I don't think he would have looked your way. I was going to reach out to Timmons, but I prayed about it and decided to hand the whole thing over to you. If you do reach out to Timmons, and things go well, I'd be honored if you'd let me do an exclusive."

"Thank you Tom I really appreciate your sensitivity on this. I will give it my vote, but there will be other voices in the room." Bill answered.

"I understand. Good luck Guys. I'll be praying for you." Tom said, before they hung up the phone.

Bill fasted for the next three days and prayed about whether to share this with Tad. He knew the answer after the first day, but he had to be sure. He discovered that it was his own fear of losing Tad that was holding him back.

Tad asked what he was praying about. He'd never seen Bill like this.

Bill just assured him that he would know soon.

It was the close of the third day, and Bill called Tad into their small kitchen and asked him to sit down. Tad was sixteen now but was still showing none of the signs of becoming a man. Bill was glad. They had enough to worry about right now. Bill looked at his son…or not. Tad's bright red curls hung loose only on the top of his head, as the rest was kept shaved short. He had three freckles on his face, and Bill wondered if soon he would long to see them.

"Son, I have some news," He began. "Remember the story that Tom was going to do after your Baptism?"

"Yeah." Tad answered.

"That's, not going to happen right now." Bill explained. "Tom emailed me three days ago, and we talked on the phone after that. During his research for the story, he talked to your mom. She told him something that caused Tom not to finish the story right now."

Tad was visibly confused and curious. "Well, what did he find?"

"He found the identity of your dad." Bill gave plenty of time for the words to sink in.

"And, at least when you were little, he was looking for you. "Your mom actually changed her name just before you were born and moved away to keep him from finding you."

"Well," Tad began. "It really doesn't matter to me. You're my dad. That's all there is to it." Tad said, sounding resolute.

"I understand that you feel that way Tad, and I appreciate it. I love you too, but this may not be as simple as that. If your biological Dad is looking for you, he will have the resources to find you. Since you're still a ward of the state, we might not have a choice.

"Well, what do you think we should do, Dad? Tad asked "I know you've been praying hard. What does God say?"

Bill's eyes teared up, proud that Tad was seeking God's will in this. "Well Tad if it's ok with you. I'd like to try to arrange a meeting. If he searched for you for all these years, then I think the guy deserves a chance. Plus, I just feel that's what God would have us to do."

"I'm just scared Dad. I finally got something good here. I don't want to mess that up."

"I feel the same way. The thing is, Son, if we're going to serve God, our decision to do right should only be determined by the question what is right, and not by all the other questions that creep into our minds. Right is always right. Circumstances are distractions to try to get our eyes off of Jesus. Remember Peter walking on the water. When Peter took his eyes off of Jesus distractions began to take him down. We have to make sure we don't let the same thing happen to us."

Tad nodded in agreement.

Bill pulled out his phone. The number he dialed was that of Timmons' lawyer, Tom Haskins.

"Haskins and Associates" came the chirpy greeting.

"Good afternoon, my name is Bill. I need to get in touch with Mr. Haskins."

"Well Good Evening sir. Can I get you to share with me the purpose of your call."

"Do me a favor ma'am tell Mr. Haskins that I need to visit with his client Mr. Timmons Concerning the name Carrie Collins. Please let Mr. Timmons know that I gave my word that I do not want anything from him. I can give my phone number."

"That won't me necessary Sir, please hold…"

Bill thought her response seemed unusual, but it wasn't like he had much experience with lawyers, especially not corporate lawyers.

"Hello, this is Thomas Haskins. How can I help you?"

"Well, sir I need to get in touch with Johnny Timmons. I understand that you represent him."

"I do. Am I to understand this is regarding one Carrie Collins? Mr. Timmons is interested to know what information you might have about her." The lawyer said.

"Yes Sir," Bill went on. "Mrs. Collins has changed her name. I know her whereabouts, but I think Mr. Timmons may be concerned about someone else that he presumes to be with Ms. Collins. If I'm correct, I think we should meet."

Mr. Haskins didn't hide his eagerness. "How soon can you be here sir? Oh, can I please get your name and number?"

Bill offered to be in Kansas City by the next morning and gave the lawyer his information. The meeting was set for 9:00 AM at the office of Mr. Haskins. Bill hung up and explained to Tad that he would be going to meet with Mr. Haskins in the morning.

However, he would not meet with Mr. Haskins or Mr. Timmons in the morning. His phone rang, not five minutes later.

"Hello," Bill answered his cell.

"Y Yes, is this Bill?" The vice stammered.

"Yes." Bill confirmed.

"This is Johnny Timmons. I understand you contacted my attorney about my son?" The stranger's voice said.

"Uh yes, I was under the understanding we were going to meet in the morning."

"Listen Sir I have been waiting seventeen years, five months, three days, and about seven hours for any word about my son. Please do not make me wait until morning."

"Mr. Timmons, I understand your position, but I really feel that we should discuss this in person." Bill explained.

"I agree. Are you located in Baymont, MO? Mr. Timmons asked in a flat business tone with a slight hint of urgency.

"Um yes. Bill answered, a bit surprised that he knew that.

"I'm sorry if this is a bit unusual, but I have a helicopter. I can be there in an hour and 15 minutes. Would you please meet me." Johnny Timmons asked.

"Um sure." Bill said.

"Great. I'll call you from the air with the details. Listen Sir, I want to thank you again. You have no idea what this means to me." The line was still open, and Bill heard the man's voice crack.

8

THREES

John Timmons

John Timmons had canceled all his appointments for the next week. This is what he had been waiting for. He couldn't believe it was finally happening....

John James Timmons's father John Paul Timmons (not after the pope) was a great man. He was a Christian of impeccable character. The young man knew he wasn't perfect, but even after living with him for 18 years, he struggled to find a single flaw that stemmed from any lack of character. John had been accused of worshiping his father, and while he didn't do this, his love for his dad was close to the level of idolatry. It was a word even he used to describe his feelings. It was not only love which could not have been more pure and sincere, but there was a level of respect that was completely unmarred. John made mistakes, but he always apologized and meant it.

Johnny spent several minutes that morning reliving the events of those fateful days that completely changed his life forever....

(Johnny was 19 years old living four hours away to attend a prestigious Tech school in Kansas City. He was invited to Greek night. It was sort of like window shopping for fraternities. Johnny had never really considered fraternity life. He felt that it wasn't really consistent with his faith or his upbringing. But he didn't think a little window shopping would hurt anything.

After an afternoon of visits, there was a big party. John had noticed one particular girl at the party. He thought she was uniquely beautiful. She was the only one who covered her body at all. Well, mostly it was just lace, but at least it was something. She was dark-headed, and easily an eight. He remembered mentioning this to a couple of the fraternity guys he was talking to. He wondered if he might be able to get her name.

Literally, the next thing he knew he was waking up with an overwhelming headache.)

John remembered that moment like it was yesterday....

I extended my arm to stretch it out. I was shocked to feel the unmistakable feeling of flesh brushing the back of my hand as I extended it. I struggled to get my eyes open. Oh, my Goodness!

Dread and horror struck my soul as I fought to focus my eyes. My worst fears mingled with my best dream came together in this moment. I could see the unmistakable Silhouette of *her face on the bed beside me!* What happened? …

John had made a commitment to keep himself pure for marriage, but now here he was in bed with a woman whose name he didn't even know. He leaned his torso off the bed, careful to keep the important stuff covered by the sheet, searching in the dim light for his clothes.

His mind raced. How could this have happened? He tried to multitask searching for the memory of how he got here. All he could remember was talking to the frat guys about her. Then one of them disappeared to get drinks. He wasn't drinking alcohol. Just punch. Oh no! the words stung in his mind. "What was in the punch?"

His full attention focused now on finding his missing clothes. That's when he heard it. That was his phone. The ringtone was "In the Garden" He wasn't even exactly sure where he was because it wasn't his room!

He was sure no one else around here had that ring tone. His heart stung with guilt as he gave up, staying covered and walked across the room completely naked. His phone was ringing from somewhere outside the room, he quietly opened the door and looked down a long hallway.

About twenty-five feet down the hallway was a sofa. As best he could tell, its where the ringtone was coming from. He felt very awkward, but he made his way quietly down the hall towards the sofa. As he approached the sofa on the left side of the hall, he noticed the space opening up to the right. It was a kitchen. All of a sudden, he froze.

He heard voices in the kitchen. Female voices! There he stood completely naked in a public hallway, feet from his clothes, and there were strange women right around the corner. He quickly made his way back to the room he had come out of.

When he opened the door, his racing heart stopped. She was awake. She must have seen the horror on his face.

"It's ok," she said. "I'm not the jealous type."

Johnny wasn't sure what to do, should he get back into bed next to the woman to cover up with the sheet. Or oh forget it. He was here now.

"Listen, I don't know what happened last night, but I really need my clothes and there are people in the kitchen. "

"Ok, so you just came from out there, why didn't you get them?" she asked flatly.

"Oh, you don't understand, I've never done anything like this before. I don't even remember your name. Oh, I'm sorry. I'm just kind of freaking out here."

"Wow. I was told you liked me. And you sure seemed to enjoy yourself last night."

"I have no idea what happened last night! I was talking to some frat guys about you being pretty, one of them brings me some punch, and the next thing I know I'm waking up here."

"Punch! You drank the punch!? Everyone knows that's spiked with "inhibition inhibitors.""

"Well, it worked! Oh, my goodness! I was not going to do this." he said, trying to keep his panicky voice down.

"I was not going to do this, listen, would you please just go down there and bring me my clothes?"

He sat down on the bed.

She began to rub his back. "you're so tense baby. Maybe I should help ease your tension a bit." Her hand gently trailed from his shoulders down the center of his back, to give her meaning. He knew he should have recoiled but he didn't.

It seemed like the instant that decision went unmade, his body began to respond to her touch. She was behind him on the bed now, and he knew if he got up, she would see it. So, he just sat there, Unsure what to do.

She continued to rub his shoulders and caress his skin, and his body continued to respond with electrical shocks shooting through his skin.

"You know, this was my first time ever being with a red head. I always wondered if all their hair was red." Her face was right above his shoulder now, and her hand was sliding down his bicep.

He was still hesitating, but his resistance was quieting. All at once he snatched the top sheet off the bed, wrapped himself and was out in the hall in a flash. He grabbed his clothes off the sofa, found a restroom just past the kitchen, and quickly dressed. He left the sheet in the bathroom, carried his shoes, and found a stairwell. He just went down. Once he was on the street, he could tell he was in the sorority house next door to the venue that housed the party. He found his car, and remembering the phone call, locked himself in his car as he checked his phone.

He had three missed calls from his mother. He struggled to compose himself while he waited for the phone to connect on the other end.

"Johnny, honey, it's your dad. He's been in an accident." Her voice trailed off.

"Mom, please focus. Tell me what's happened." The sick and sinking feeling in the pit of his stomach seemed to get very heavy. And he could feel his throat tighten. He opened the door, thinking he would vomit.

"Honey, we don't know if he's going to make it." He's at Mercy Hospital in the ICU. You need to get here as fast as you can but be safe."

Johnny sped to his dorm, ran in, showered (hoping to wash the guilt away to no avail), and dressed. When he reached the hospital. It was too late. John Paul Timmons was with The Lord. Johnny struggled to focus. He resolved that his father would want him to finish school.

They say things happen in threes. Well, the third thing that rocked Johnny's world would happen about two months to the day after the funeral.

Johnny was studying in the technology lab when a girl (he didn't recognize) walked right up to him and smacked him square across his face.

Stunned, his hand instinctively covered the place where the blow had landed. His jaw dropped, and he stammered "H-Hey, what's th-that for?"

"That's for Carrie you idiot!" she screamed, walking away.

(Johnny still didn't know the girl's name, and he hadn't seen her since that morning in the sorority house.)

"Who's Carrie?" He yelled after his assailant.

"You dense…" she called him a series of names that didn't matter after her next words. "She's the girl that's carrying your son!

Her words landed like a dagger to the chest. He jumped up and ran after her. He caught up with her as she exited the lab.

"Hey, wait a minute, you can't just say something like that and then run away!" His voice was cracking. "What do you mean she's carrying my son?" His brain is slowly catching up. "It was only one night. I don't remember anything about it. Where is she? How can I find her? Please tell me she hasn't…" His voice trailed off unable to say the words.

"Well, you idiot! "The girl said with unrelenting intensity. "It only takes one deposit to open an account! I don't know where she went! She's gone! Don't you stupid boys know how to cover you junk!?" The girl yelled at him.

"Wait! I have to find her. I need her name and number. I have to find her, please. I'll do anything." His voice was rising in pitch and volume.

The girl grabbed Johnny's hand and wrote the name Carrie Collins. And a phone number. "You stupid boy there's nothing you can do! You don't even know how to stretch rubber. This is her number. Her family is from Kansas."

Johnny went to the sorority president and managed to get Carries permanent address. Six days later he made the four-hour drive to Pratt, Kansas. To find Carrie.

At 620 Country Club Road He found Pratt County Estates, a trailer park community. He knocked on fifteen doors before someone recognized Carrie's name, but twenty-three before anyone would show him where she lived.

It was a 12-year-old girl on her bike that told Johnny where to find her. He thanked the girl and gave her a $5 bill.

The mobile home was brown and white. Three broken steps at the end of a mud path led to the porch that Johnny concluded was honestly a bit scary. He had just passed an old junk car rusting out on blocks next to the broken steps.

"Carrie" Johnny said when she answered the door.

"What are you doing here?" She asked shaking her head. "So much for friends."

"Come on Sammy, let's go outside." She said to someone inside the house.

A very dirty little boy followed her out the door.

"He's my kid brother. What's your name again, never mind I don't care. I suppose you drove all the way to Pratt to make sure I get rid of it, so it can't come back to ruin your perfect little life?" Carry said never even looking at John.

"No, I came all the way to Pratt to make sure you don't get rid of it!" John protested angrily.

"Well, what does it matter to you? You don't even remember sleeping with me!" She said, rage and sarcasm ruling her tone.

"Well, I just don't believe its right to murder a baby just because he or she may be inconvenient." John said.

"I may not have intended for this to happen, but I still made the decision to go to that party. I made the decision to drink frat boys' punch, and regardless of what may have helped it along If that baby is mine, I want to take care of it. I want to keep it and raise it. We can do it together, we can do it separate, or I can do it by myself, but under absolutely no circumstances can we abort that baby!" John said with much less passion than he had practiced.

"Well haven't you ever heard of woman's rights? It isn't now, nor will it every be YOUR BABY until our unless I deliver it and write your name on the birth certificate." She screamed. "And if I decide to abort the baby, with no baby there's no paternity, so again. You're in luck. You don't have a baby."

Johnny was frustrated now. "You aren't Listening to me! I want the baby! It's my flesh and blood I want it!

"I know, I know. I know exactly what men want babies for! Its so they can use them and trade them, and share them, and ..." her voice cracked and trailed off.

"That's ridiculous! I don't know what you're talking about! John was yelling now. "The best thing that can ever happen to a child is for him to have a great dad!" Johnny was offended and as angry as he could ever remember being. He felt the temperature rise in his face. "My dad was the greatest man I've ever known. He never did any of that stuff! You... You're the whole reason I didn't get to tell him good-bye! Look, just promise me that you won't abort that baby! It is a human life!" His volume was falling quickly now. "It deserves to live! Truthfully, its rights are more important than ours. It didn't choose to be here. It had nothing to do with it at all!" He didn't finish before being interrupted.

"Stop calling him an it!" She snapped without thinking. Her voice and face softened. "Ok, I'm not going to abort him. I mean I thought about it. I thought it's better to abort a baby than to let him be abused… But then I started to feel him inside me. I felt him kick and flip inside me. I know he's alive."

Johnny could feel tears welling up in his eyes. "I'm going to be a dad. I'm going to have a son!"

"God gave me a son on the same day he took my dad. Don't you understand the same day that we slept together was the day my dad died? My greatest hero, my best friend…. We just have to protect him."

Johnny would not leave until Carrie promised that she would come back to KC in one week. He gave her his number and she promised to keep him posted about everything that happened.

That's the last time Johnny ever saw Carrie. When Carrie never called, he waited six more days before driving back to Pratt to find that the trailer was empty.

The little boy, Carrie's brother, had been killed by her uncle that they stayed with. Carrie ran away. Johnny had searched for Carrie and the baby every day since that one. Now, thanks to Bill Hinchum he was on his way to Baymont, MO, maybe not to meet his son, but at the very least, to meet the man who might know him.

He had worked so hard, and when he sold his app the only thing, he could think about was finally he would have the means to find his boy! He had given everyone who had anything to do with his business affairs explicit instructions that if anyone ever called and mentioned the name Carrie Collins, they were to be given the absolute highest priority.

Johnny had been given permission to land in the field next to the school where medevac choppers often do. Bill would meet him there. There was nothing to do for the last thirty minutes but pray.

He needed wisdom. He needed grace in the eyes of Mr. Hinchum. He needed mercy to find that his son was well. He had prayed for him everyday since he knew of his conception, but he had been plagued with nightmares of terrible things happening to him. He was always chasing him, but he could never seem to catch up.

9

ANSWERED PRAYERS

Bill

Bill received a text from Johnny Timmons That his chopper would set down about 6:45PM in the field next to the school. He had already talked to Tad and explained that he would wait out the meeting at his Aunt Sandy's. Sandy, like many of the people closest to Bill, was not his sister. Neither was Sandy's husband Bill's brother. Now they *were* family, but nothing nearly so close, but it didn't matter. Bill always said blood is thicker than water, but love is much thicker than blood. That had certainly proved true in his life.

He dropped Tad off at Sandy's twenty minutes before his Rendezvous with the millionaire father of his son. It would take ten minutes to get to the school.

The chopper was on site when Bill pulled into the parking lot beside the school. He waived at the chopper as he got out of his ford explorer. Before it ever reached the ground, Johnny Timmons leapt from the open door.

He shook hands with Bill as the two men made their way back towards Bill vehicle and away from the noise of the chopper blades.

"I'll be glad to buy your gas if you want to drive. Let's find somewhere to grab a booth and something to drink so we can talk." John said, in a business tone.

Bill nodded and led the way to the truck. "So, tell me about John Timmons, tech mogul."

"If it's all the same, I'd like to tell you about John Timmons the pastor." John responded.

Bill was immediately intrigued. He nodded. John Timmons was my father. He was the pastor of the Bible Baptist Church of Cassandra, Missouri in the far northeastern corner of the state for 47 years. He was the closest thing to perfect next to Jesus Christ himself. I was his only son and namesake. I'll never be him, but I strive every day to do right by his legacy. I have made a lot of mistakes, Mr. Hinchum, but I assure you, I have been searching for my son since the moment I found out he was conceived. He was conceived the last night my father was alive. It was because of the events that lead to his conception that I didn't get to say goodby to my dad, my hero and best friend."

The younger man was clearly fighting extraordinarily strong emotions and Bill's experience made him easy to read. At the Dairy Queen, Bill took a seat across from Johnny and pulled a tablet from his satchel that he had preloaded with the information from Tom.

"What'll you drink John?" Bill asked sliding out of his booth.

John waved his hand dismissing the request, so Bill just ordered two Pepsis. When he returned to the table the other man was in tears. Shaking his head and trying his best to read the account of Tad's life between swipes of his napkin.

Bill was amazed how 13 years of a boy's life could be consumed in five minutes from the face of a tablet. It was a credit to Tom's concise writing and impeccable organization. As soon as the thought entered Bill's mind, it was replaced by the volumes that the page wouldn't tell him.

He remembered the file that he had been given at the DFS office the day he met Tad. He realized he'd made the same fatal error that the workers there had. He had no right to tell Tad's story. He knew in his spirit what needed to happen next, but he was made even more certain by what he witnessed.

Johnny slid from his seat out the side and around the back to the walkway that led to a trash receptacle. There he fell to his knees and began to weep. A few minutes later he rose from the floor, wiped his face, and sat back down.

"I have been praying for this day for fourteen years, three months, two weeks, and two days. He was conceived March 3rd. I found out about him on May 13th. I have prayed every day from that day to this that my boy would be safe. That he would be cared for, and that God would find the grace to let me see him and be a father to him.

"There are a few details that you need to know, John. First of all, when I agreed to take Tad into my home, I agreed that I would never stop wanting him, pursuing him, fighting for him, and regardless if someone takes him from me, I will be his family forever. I meant what I said.

Tad has been calling me Dad for about six months now. Since the day I was privileged to help him call upon Christ as his savior. I love him and he loves me. Tad has been through a lot of traumas. He has experienced abandonment, rejection, and trauma all his life until now.

He is terrified that now that he's finally found something good...." Bill's words trailed off as he fought to keep his own composure. "That something will happen to mess that up." I would have adopted Tad on day one, the day I brought him home. That was my commitment, but social services and the courts have yet to release him for adoption.

Meaning that whatever happens from here will have to go through the state." I just want you to be incredibly careful here. I know that you have a great deal of emotion invested in this, I've seen that. So do I, but this cannot be about you and me. This has got to be about Tad.

No matter what you have suffered to this point, it can never be about that. He is the victim in all this. He has been through so much. Finally having people that love him and are committed to him should not cause him more heartache than when he had no one!"

Johnny nodded. "The last thing in the world that I would ever want to do is to hurt him. I love him. I've loved his since before he was born."

Bill's voice was firm and level. "Then don't make decisions for him. Not about this. Let him get to know you, and then if he wants to pursue that, then move at his pace."

Johnny nodded. "I promise. I promise."

With that, Bill stood. "Then its time to meet our son." John froze unable to believe his ears. He wanted to ask how, why; but he didn't care. Bill saw the questions in his face as he turned to head for the door. As he walked, he recounted the story of file, and how only Tad deserved to tell his story. Then they drove in silence to Sandy's.

Tad was sitting on the porch when they pulled into the driveway. Bill noticed again the striking resemblance between Johnny and Tad. He was the spitting image of his dad. This was a happy ending brewing, but Bill knew it would be awfully hard for him. He repeated the same request he'd made of John..." It's not about you Bill!" He thought.

Tad walked to the driver's side of the truck and gave Bill a big hug as soon as the door opened. He took a long look at Johnny, and Bill could tell… he saw it too.

Johnny was fighting tears as he followed them to the porch.

On the Porch Bill took the lead, introducing the other two.

"Tad this is your father" careful to use the term that he never used to refer to himself and that Tad never called him. It seemed appropriate too since it does refer to the familiar relationship more so than dad which refers to the emotional relationship. Right now, he was satisfied that this was good enough.

"Johnny, this is Tad."

"I'm sorry, but I need to talk you Jesus right now." He prayed out loud crying praising, praising God for answering prayers. Careful not to mention what prayers. He didn't want to make his son nervous after all. He did not know their prayer culture.

Tad…

Tad had made up his mind when dad texted him that he was bringing John Timmons here. He would give Dad a hug right away, so this Timmons would know who his dad was. He had trouble taking his eyes off Johnny, though. He looked so much like him. It was like looking in a mirror that showed what you would look like when you were older. I mean it was really weird. He wanted to trust his dad, and for sure God, but this is really scary!

When the guy prayed, Tad wondered if he meant it or if he was just acting because he knew we were Christian. He decided he'd just have to wait and see.

The three talked on the porch into the night. Johnny telling the story of his own father. He told the story of how he met and knew his mother, not concerned about withholding details, since he didn't have any. He told of how he had prayed for God to show him a way to find his son. Then there was the app. Johnny was careful not to mention any dollar amounts.

Then Bill called. It was an answer to the prayer prayed for fourteen years, three months, two weeks, and two days. He explained this, and Johnny's eyes were being whipped, but so were Tad's.

Then Tad and Bill took turns telling stories of their time together. As the evening wore on, it became clear to Bill that, not tonight, but someday Tad would go to live with his father. He was a good man and he certainly had wanted him. He also saw the potential for a long friendship between the three. They were like-minded, kindred spirits. Johhny spent the night on Bill's couch in the apartment, and it dawned on Bill that Johnny didn't seem much all that like a millionaire or like he imagined one might be.

Over the next months Bill and Tad would be picked up in the chopper (the landing strip moving to the field next to the apartment.) many times. They flew up north to meet Johnny and Tad's family. That is where Bill first met Debra.

Debra fell in love with the heart that Bill had for helping kids. Really, everyone did. That's why Johnny created the Construction Trust. This was a trust account that he had given to Bill to purchase property and build buildings to support the vision of Home.

After a few discussions about construction, though Johnny made one stipulation. Bill was not to design. Bill, Johnny determined, was too modest.

A professional architect was employed to design all the buildings. Bill was to give specs, but the final design was up to the design committee. That's why the entire campus of *The Home* looked like something out of colonial times. Even if that were about to change with the new modern structure being framed on the hill.

Johnny said any facilities that would be built would need to be worthy of his son. As the months went on it became clear that the only two people Johnny would ever worship more that his father would be, of course, Jesus and Tad. In-fact before Tad moved in, Johnny still lived in the same apartment he had bought after tech school. It would simply not be big enough for Tad.

Bill had a standing invitation at the Timmons' ranch, and though he seldom used it, he also had a cherry red H255 twin turbine rotorcraft helicopter that waited in a hangar at the municipal airport just in case Bill needed to get to Tad faster than one of his 2021 model year people mover vans could get him there.

The biggest thing that came out of that chapter of Bill's story was Tad getting reunited with a great family that had been longing for him since prior to his birth.

The other thing which was just as big was the establishment of the trust which had now helped scores of kids find a home forever and ever, and many more find hope and rescue from hellish circumstances.

Ever House, was where Bill's son Moses and his wife Jen Lived. They cared for thirteen charges. These were the boys that had been with Bill the Longest. In fact, Bill lived there right up until Ever House was finished three years ago. Moses had been back and forth.

When Bill's wife, Carla, put him out fifteen years ago, he thought his life was over. The ashes of that devastation eventually gave way to the dream of a home.

The two had lived in the home they inherited from her parents, so naturally when the relationship ended, she kept the house. Bill found himself homeless, and that was a feeling he hadn't felt in some time. Since he himself had been a charge tossed to and from at the whim of strangers,

He found himself not only with no home, but with very little family left to speak of. The experience brought him back to a dream he had never been quite able to forget or realize since those early days of his own youth.

He thought of Moses. As he looked out over the hills separating his current location from Ever House. Moses, Bill's son had gone away to Bible College and to the military before coming to spend the Summer of 2015 with Bill at home. That's when he met Jen. Jennifer had come to live with Bill as the only girl to ever live in Ever Home. She and her brother John had been through a terrible ordeal.

Bill was no fool. He knew there was absolutely no way he could keep this place going without a really great team, so at the bequest of that team, Jennifer joined the family, and Home became something Bill had always dreamed for it to be, a place where siblings could stay together.

"In the early days" He'd said once in a lecture, "I listened to everyone tell me how it needed to be done. You, know you can't have boys *and* girls on the same campus, much less in the same house." Well hog wash!" he exclaimed. He had discovered that it could be done, it just needed to be done thoughtfully.

10. What's Unseen

Mark, was a very handsome young man, muscular, and well-spoken; though his voice was naturally soft. He was dressed in blue jeans and a polo shirt as he made his way up the sidewalk from Ever House. He wore white sneakers and carried a tan backpack over his right shoulder.

Bill noticed his approach and returned his notebook to its place, stood, and greeted him with a gentle hug.

"Hey bud, what's happening?"

"Well," the two sat down after Bill refilled his coffee cup. "I was thinking about going to prom." Mark answered tentatively. He waited for Bill to respond to no avail.

"Who is she?" His voice was low and level.

Mark smiled sheepishly. "Her name is Pam. She's in my history class."

"Yes..." Bill answered, "and what are your intentions?"

"I don't know, Dad, she's a really great girl. She's super smart, and she leads in prayer in FCA.

She dresses conservatively, and yesterday I walked up on her singing "Amazing Grace" I thought I had died and gone to Heaven. I've been praying about it, and I just feel like I gotta get to know her."

"You're thinking about her a lot. Did that have anything to do with your math grade?" Bill inquired. There was no judgement in his voice just calm, quiet and purposeful.

"It has to do with me feeling like I can't think about anything. I used to talk to her all the time, but now I can't string two words together without stammering and stuttering. Dad, you know, I am usually a really good talker. I just lose it every time I get near her. And when I'm not near her, I'm thinking about her. Do you think I'm losing it? Am I turning into a stalker or something?"

"Well congratulations Mark! This one has nothing to do with being a foster, dealing with your past, managing your PTSD, or any of the rest. This is the most normal, everyday problem you've ever had in your life. It's called a crush, Mark, and it sounds to me like you've got rather good taste. When is prom?"

"I don't know. May, I think." Mark said.

"When are you suppressed to register for prom?"

"I don't know," Mark answered.

"Alright. I'm not going to give an answer about prom just yet. Get the rest of the information. In the meantime, I think you need to ask her out "

"What? I know you don't like dating for guys and girl my age." Mark asked his shock evident.

"Cool your jets there man. I'm not suggesting alone. I'm open to the possibility that The Lord may be leading you in this and not just hormones. However, I am still not going to put you in a compromising situation. You may invite her here to study any time between 4 and 7 on weekdays. You'll do said studying in the den or the dining room, so you can offer her a drink. You can also invite her to dinner with a chaperone."

"Oh Dad, Debra is always saying how much trouble girls are. I'm afraid she'll be mean."

"I don't think Debra would ever be mean, but she is very protective of you and doesn't want you to make a mistake. However, I was thinking of Jen. She's younger and she's probably a bit more understanding of your position and the young lady's."

"Oh, that's perfect! She is the perfect chaperone. Oh" He stopped, paused, and started again; the excitement completely gone from his voice. "Do I have to ask her dad?"

"Do I need to answer that?" Bill asked.

"I know, only if she's worth it, and if she's not; I shouldn't be wasting her time. Ok" Mark said, dread, then resolution settling into his voice.

"Now, about that math test?" Bill asked.

"Ah! I'm not really worried about that. I have a feeling once I figure out what to do about Pam, I'll have no more trouble concentrating on Geometry."

Sandy was delivering their breakfast, and they fell quiet for a few minutes.

"Bill, do you think kids like me can be good dads and husbands after everything we've been through? I'm just so afraid of becoming like my dad or worse my stepdad." Mark asked between bites of biscuit.

"Well, do you think I'm a good dad?"

"Well yeah! I guess your such a good dad that I forget that you were a foster before. But didn't you get divorced?" His voice was reverent and hesitant. Not willing to offend.

"Yes, I did. Son, I'm not going to tell you that my past didn't contribute to the collapse of my marriage. I think what allowed that to happen most, was that I wasn't embracing and processing it; that I didn't understand trauma enough to respect the impact it could have on my life. I had not sought treatment for my PTSD. I was so busy trying to leave my past behind that I didn't notice when it snuck up on me.

I was also so desperate for a family that I was willing to accept it in whatever form it took, even if that was not very healthy. That's the number one mistake that young people who have experienced trauma and abandonment can make…. To set their standards so low and accept a bad situation over being alone. I'm not going to lie. It is extremely hard to think through all that with all the emotions that are present in a relationship. If the relationship has become physical, then there are added chemical components that make it almost impossible.

So, if you keep The Lord first, do things His way, and listen to those who love you I definitely think you can. In every relationship, you have to have boundaries for your own behavior and those of others that are hard lines that you simply cannot allow to be crossed." Bill said.

Mark was nodding his head and glanced at his phone. "I still have time to catch the bus. Thanks Dad. I know you're super busy. I appreciate you taking the time to talk. "

"Mark if the day ever comes when I can't make the time to talk to you, it'll be time to make some real adjustments. I love you too."

"Hey, I thought Cole was moving in last night. Is everything OK with him? Court go alright?"

"Ah yeah. He actually helped me rescue a new boy yesterday, so I'm keeping him there for an extra day or two to help Jeff get acclimated."

"Awesome! I rely like Cole. I'm glad to have another little brother. I heard we had another newbie come in last night. How's he doing?"

"You know Mark, he reminds me of you. He ran away from his stepdad after a bad exchange. We're trying to locate his mother right now. You know better than any how that road can go." Bill responded his voice emanating compassion.

"Well, they said he was a cat three, so I wondered. Hey, you know you're a hero to all of us, don't you? We love you, Dad. All of us. Every time we get a newbie, but especially a cat 3 I pray, and I go back to the first time I saw you. I couldn't have imagined it, but my life is probably as good now as it was bad then. That's all you. You're more than a dad to us. You're…. Well, it was easy to understand what a savior was, cause I'd already seen one. When you walked into that room that day. I was lost, so scared, and so mad. I hate to think what would have happened if you hadn't showed up."

The two stood and embraced. It was Bill who was crying now. "You silver tongued devil." He said as he patted his shoulders to emphasize his words. "I love you son. It was a good day for me too. It was a good day for me too."

The embrace ended and Mark turned and headed back towards and ever house. Bill chugged the rest of his coffee and headed towards Now house. He stole one last glance at the panorama that had become Home. He took one deep breath of shear satisfaction and whispered a prayer…. "It's time to face what Miracles that are in the Making today...Thank you Lord!"

The next few hours were spent on a variety of tasks, tending to Jeff, facilitating his meeting with Chief and Susie; but it really turned into passing the time before Tad arrived. When he did, Bill couldn't have been more pleased. The Tall man with the broad shoulders and the bright red hair couldn't have been a more striking fella or a more welcomed sight.

After Chief and Susie had left, Jeff stayed with Cole as they went through their normal day of school and chores. Bill has made a very unusual return to his coffee porch. Tad came strolling down the path from And Ever House.

Bill rose and met him halfway and the two embraced. "Gosh it's good to see you, Kid!" Bill said.

"Ah, whatever Pops, you probably don't even remember my name. What with you getting old and having four hundred and twenty-two little angels out here, you probably don't even know who I am. I'm surprised they even let me through the gate." Tad teased.

"You stinking little turd, I'll never forget your name. Slash!" Bill said, pretending to be brash."

The two just started laughing.

"Yeah, I asked Deborah on the way in if I could borrow a paring knife, but she said something about all the knife drawers having thumbprint locks? Not sure what that was about?" Tad joked.

"I don't know if I ever told you, the first little turd I had. He agreed that we should help other kids. Then he went out and slit all four tires on my truck." Bill said.

"I bet you shipped his little butt back too quick to talk about Huh?"

"Nope, just got more stubborn than ever that I'd never send him back. your punishment for that, a life sentence...stuck with me." Bill said.

They laughed again, and Bill's heart ached for the old days when he got to see Tad every day. He had grown into a good man. Bill smiled. If he really had only adopted one son, he would have been an excellent choice. It is still true, the devil attacks hardest the individuals for whom God has the most in store. That's something he'd picked up years ago, when he was serving in junior church. Those that were the most distracted, the most hyper, the most disruptive…those were the ones to watch. Bill's mind went right to the scripture…the Lord's message to Paul, "My grace is sufficient (enough) for you, for my strength is made perfect (complete) in weakness." That principle was so true. The Lord does seem to use the least likely candidates, to bring glory and praise back to Himself.

"Hey, have you been here since they broke ground on the new space stations over here?" Bill asked, as the two rose and moved down the path towards the new construction.

"Nope. Dad just said they were building me a house." As soon as he said it, I knew it would be elaborate. He doesn't know how to go small when it comes to me." Tad said.

"He's a good picture of your heavenly father. He doesn't like to go small either." Bill said.

Tad was already nodding. Both men marveled at the immense structures that rose before them. The path took them beyond And Ever House, then off to the west. They did have the appearance of something space age with all their steel and glass against the colonial style of the rest of the houses.

Bill was amazed at the progress that had been made in just a few weeks. The walls were up and the windows in. It looked like this morning they would actually walk through the front doors. As Bill looked at them now, they didn't look as out of place as they had before. They were both red Brick on three sides. They were connected by a huge atrium between, that looked out on the Hills to the East and the Houses to the west.

"Explain again why dad decided to build this? He just told me it would give me a place to stay when I come over someday and bring my wife and kids." Tad inquired.

"Well, it first began rumbling when Moses came home from the service. He shared a room with me. That was fine, but it got me to look ahead. I knew then, that we were going to have a problem. If I promise these kids to always be here for them, then what happens if they need to fall back on us after they go out on their own? Forever means forever. I would never have turned Moses away, and I could never turn any of you away either. I knew we were going to have to do something.

We were just too crowded in the houses to do it there. You were my oldest bonus kid and you've got support, so I knew I had time for that. We needed the shelter desperately, and when that came about, Mo decided to stay; those things just became more urgent. The timing is going to be perfect. I have three guys graduating this year, so those quarters are going to be needed."

Tad nodded as they approached the front door of the atrium. The room was enormous. Forty-foot ceilings, the expanse was eighty-foot square.

"This room will be the common ground and the title track for the whole project. The room is combination of living room, sitting room, cafeteria, and meeting space. Both houses will serve as guest quarters with one- and two-bedroom suites. This will be for the fallback kids. It'll also serve as staff housing as the program continued to grow." Bill explained.

"Imagined doing dinners here to get everyone together under one roof. We'll do Sunday evening church here as well."

When Bill mentioned this, and the future need for a functioning church on site, Tad stopped. His face told Bill he was taking a trip.

Bill didn't ask, but he could tell Tad was just a little distracted the rest of the day.

They descended the stairs from peeking at one of the "apartments," as Tad called them, teasing Bill that he would need to "fall back" as soon as possible. "Everyone needs a vacation," he said.

That's when Bill noticed Cole standing at the bottom of the stairs.

Tad noticed him too, and spoke first,

"Well, hello, sir, I don't believe we've met. I'm Tad," he said.

"Hey, wait," Cole looked at Bill. "Are you that Tad?" He asked stammering a bit.

"Yep, they used to call me slash." Tad said, pretending he knew what Cole was thinking in a playful tone.

Cole shot Tad a brief confused look in response to his last comment. "Is this the Tad that you said started everything with you and rescuing boys?" He was looking at Bill now.

The two reached the bottom of the stairs and Bill introduced them. "Tad, I'd like you to meet your newest brother, Cole."

"Hey Bro. I'm sorry I won't be around too much to change your diapers and help you get into all kinds of trouble. "

Cole started to smile before turning his attention back to Bill. "Dad Ms. Deborah asked me to come deliver a message. The Chief called and has information for you. She said you had company, so you'd never answer your phone."

"Would you boys like to visit for a minute while I take this call?" Bill asked. He had told the two a bit about the other, and both had interest in meeting. Bill had been praying for some time that God would call Tad back to help him. He was working in the youth ministry and had expressed frustration at not being able to have the level of impact with the kids that he really felt was necessary.

He left the two after a nod from each, and they started chattering like they'd known each other for years. That was Tad's gift, and after yesterday... Bill admitted, was quickly becoming Cole's as well.

"Hello, Chief, I'm sorry Tad's here. I was showing him around at the Common Ground. What's up?" Bill said.

"Well, we found the boy's mother. She checked into Mercy Hospital this morning. I don't know how. She's busted up pretty good. He busted about all her ribs, she's got a broken arm, and she's spitting up blood. She knew if she came in, they'd call me.

She's asking about Jeff. I told her we have him and he is safe. You know what I can't figure out, Bill? This lady used to run some of the largest hotels in the country. She has a master's degree in business administration. He's got her reduced to staying at home serving as his punching bag. I'm going to lean on her pretty hard to press charges. She'd like to see the boy." Chief concluded.

"Can we tell her we can't bring Jeff until Jim is in custody? We do need to be able to guarantee his safety." Bill inquired.

"I was already thinking the same thing. I'll go back in and propose it now. I think you'd like her Bill. She's a Prayer".

"The question we must answer now Chief, is, Is she a doer? Jeff is going to need her to do something different than what she did to get him here."

"Yes, that's absolutely right Bill. I'll let you know when I have more."

Bill walked back to his two bonus sons, the most and least recent additions to his growing clan. He stopped short to watch them for a moment, taking time to seal the image in his mind. He loved both boys, and something seemed so natural about them being together. He could have watched them all day. The two of them seemed to summarize God's miraculous work in Bill's life, the past and the present, the young and the older now, the reunited and the adopted, the youth director and the youth. They looked remarkable enough on the surface, but knowing the miracles... The traumas and the dramas, the victories, and the triumphs ...that God has and is working out beneath the surface; just out of sight: those are the true miracles in the making! The Cedars of Lebanon, the Great Redwoods of California; the structures growing before me have the potential to grow stronger, to live longer; if they make the right choices and trust the right person. They also are a far more beautiful picture of grace, to those who are willing to see the whole picture.

THE END OF
THE KID WHISPERER
SERIES, BOOK ONE

To learn more about the characters you've met in *Miracles in the Making* (Bill Hinchum, Cole, Jeff, Mark, Jen, Tad and more) and to learn how predicting your course as you follow The Lord can be a lot like trying to plot a straight line through a tornado, or driving an old pickup down an Ozark Mountain highway, look for the continuing trials and triumphs of...

EPILOGUE

NOW AND
FOREVER HOME

A preview to The Kid Whisperer Series, Book 2

As Bill stood watching Cole and Tad in the Meeting Place, his phone still in his hand after hanging up with the chief. His thoughts were interrupted by the vibration of a call.

"Hey Bill" The voice belonged to chief. "She's pressing charges. Said Jim's abuse of her has been steadily escalating, but he had never touched the boy before. Says that's crossing a line. She never wants to see him again. She's concerned about Jeff and her situation. She says she's going to need to find a shelter or something, because their place is rented and she doesn't have a job. Name's Cindy. She's at least talking the right talk. We're picking Jim up at work now, and I'm going to get a search warrant for the house."

The two men finished their call, and Bill whispered a prayer for Cindy, before joining the young men in front of him. He prayed for her healing and for resolve to stick by her decision an for her to do a better job of protecting Jeff in the future.

He would visit Cindy the next day in the hospital. He could tell every breath and certainly every word cause the woman physical pain, due to her injuries. However, what Bill was looking for was any signs that her situation and that of her son was causing her emotional pain. When she asked about Jeff, Bill did not hold back about his condition when they found him.

"Ma'am you do realize that Jeff actually had drywall embedded in his scalp where his head hit the wall. If he hadn't run, I'm afraid you would be planning a funeral today."

There were the tears. He felt bad, but he needed them to come. He was genuinely afraid for Jeff. He had not said this to be cruel, but because he was sure once she healed, they would return Jeff to her. Bill had spent the much of the morning with him discussing the escalating violence that had both mother and son terrified for their lives. He needed to know weather he should push Sussie to let the two visit, something they both wanted, or if he should resist this.

Jeff had cried and begged to see his mother when Bill told him they had found her and that she was in the hospital. Sussie wasn't sure that was a good idea just yet, and procedures prevented it anyway. Bill promised Jeff to check on his mother and report back to him on her condition. He would continue to check in on her a couple times a week for the next couple of weeks as she recovered. Over that time, he answered her concerns about her son, and explained what kind of place he was in.

Jim was arrested on a myriad of chargers ranging from domestic assault, Felony child abuse, child endangerment, and several others. It was also discovered that he had a history of this kind of abuse. He was not going to get out of jail any time soon.

It was 19 days after Jeff had come home when the court convened for the "emergency hearing" they determined that Jeff needed to stay in custody until his mother could show that she could provide a safe and stable living environment for him. Bill accepted responsibility for supervising the visits between the two in the meantime.

Outside the courtroom, Bill greeted Cindy. He could see she was pretty emotional over the proceedings. Bill asked her if she'd like to come over now to see Jeff. The woman who was still noticeably sore from her injuries began to sob.

"I appreciate that Mr. Henham, but the truth is I have no way to get out there, and I have to figure out what to do about my living arrangements since the month-to-month lease on my house was up a week ago. The landlord is being gracious because I was in the hospital, but I'm honestly not sure what to do."

Bill listened intently reading her face for any indication of insincerity. He saw none. "I'll tell you what," He began with the same measured, controlled voice that he used with the kids, why don't I give you a ride out to our place. You can visit with Jeff; see where and how he is. Then I'll give you a ride back to town after."

Suspicion flashed across Cindy's thin face as the question lingered in her eyes.

Bill immediately saw the question she was thinking, and quickly raised his hands in a gesture of surrender and answered before she asked. "Hey, no strings. I give you my word."

It's not that Bill didn't notice Cindy, even with the broken nose and the disappearing bruise on her cheek, she was tall, well built (not thin, but certainly not heavy at least not noticeably so. She was dressed elegantly enough in her burgundy business suit with the wide collar and flared legs. It was made of a light material that caught the wind. He noticed. He just couldn't see past the vision of Jeff's broken face every time he saw her.

She came to visit Jeff. She invited to stay for lunch and she, Jeff, and Jenn took their lunch at the picnic table outside now house. The gentle breeze made for a beautiful day.

Bill and Cindy were back in the van now headed back to town now, and tears began to flow unabated. "He looks so good Bill. His smile, she choked on her words and began to sob. A few moments later she regained some of her composure. "I just haven't seen that smile in some time. The gleam in his eye, that somehow, I hadn't noticed had faded. It's back," Tears again. "What I mean is," she started again and seemed to gain strength and confidence as she went this time. "I want you to know that I really appreciate you all being there and taking care of Jeff. I know you must think I'm a horrible mother, and I honestly agree with you most of the time now. I know its probably normal for parents to feel some resentment towards those who care for their children, but I want you to know that I don't."

"I see how much everybody cares, and I'm just so grateful. I'm not sure how I could ever have fallen into the dark pit that my life had become. Jeff isn't the only one who has got his spark back. I'm not sure when I lost it. I'm not sure in what moment I surrendered myself, but as I sat there and listened to Jeff chatter about you and Cole, Tristan, and Deb. He smiled, and I felt something return. I'm not sure what my future holds, but I know by the grace of God, I'm not finished like I had started to think I was." She let her voice trail off after becoming hesitant again.

As Bill listened, he was keenly aware of another voice that had been talking to him for a few weeks. His offer to supervise Cindy's visits and her visit to the home today was very much about Jeff, but Bill had also begun to gain an understanding over the past couple of weeks visiting with Cindy. It was sort of like looking at a map in the dark by the light of a tiny pen light. Like the more time passed the more the little circle of light moved across the map revealing a previously unseen destination.

Cindy was, or had been a hotel administrator. Her bachelor's degree was in hospitality and her master in business administration. He had learned this from the chief, but also from his conversations with Cindy as he visited with her in the hospital.

He was going to need someone to oversee the management and operation of a thirty-six-unit facility for his fall-back kids. He was fairly certain this is what The Lord was doing. He offered a silent prayer now. "Was this the time to ask?" He knew it was.

"Cindy, I know you need a place to stay, and you need a job. Your experience in hospitality is extensive. I believe, in time you could find a very lucrative career in the hotel industry again. However, I have a lead for you. You know the new facility we are constructing on the property? Well, it is comprised of the Atrium and the thirty-six suites that we are constructing for staff and for our fall-back kids. The atrium will house a fairly well-equipped commercial style kitchen and some amenities. I've been praying that The Lord would send me the right person to manage that project. It's not a five-star retreat and certainly won't have the salary, but it could come with a two-bedroom suit. One of them could be ready temporarily within a week. You could provide direction on the finishings for more permanent quarters, if you like." Bill said.

Cindy's eyes seemed to dance, despite her attempt to hold her expression. Her head dropped and after a few seconds she answered with a question. "How much do you get paid, Mr. Henham?"

Bill was taken aback by the question. It honestly surprised him. However, he took a deep breath and considered carefully before offering as honest an answer as he could in his measured and warm tone.

"Well, I live on campus in one of the houses. I take all my meals there, and I carry *The Home* bank card for any expenses. My needs are met. I do not have a bank account of my own. I report sixty thousand dollars in income to the IRS for tax purposes, and the accounting department provides me with the necessary documents each year."

She did not immediately respond to this information. She began to speak slowly. "I do have to get back to work, and hospitality is something I love. I really like the customer service aspect of the field. One of the reasons I got mixed up with Jim in the first place was because I wanted, well. I thought Jeff needed to be around men. I obviously am not very good at choosing men. However, I believe I see you, Mr. Henham. I believe you are a good man. I see the way you watch and consider before you respond. I see how those boys; my boy loves you. They revere you. I now know you do not do what you do for money. You've already told me you do not own the property. You do not take a salary. I do not believe you are a pervert. You do not appear to be a tyrant or control freak. Are you a cult leader?" She asked. Her tone was completely unwavering?

That was the first time he'd ever been asked that, but Bill did not feel the question was an attack. He calmly responded, "Well I attend Riverview Baptist Church where I have been a member for the past seven years. I was a Baptist pastor and youth pastor for several years. I am in full agreement with the doctrine and teachings of our church. Do you think I'm a cult leader?"

"To be honest, Mr. Henham, I have no idea what you are. I have been praying for you and for your work since I first learned that Jeff was with you. I do need a place to stay. How would you consider a probationary period? It would give me a chance to see what you're all about and get out of my current situation."

"I would, and though they all work hand in hand the Gathering place is a separate nonprofit entity, so you could start working and move in without it affecting Jeff's placement as long as you agree not to take unsupervised visits until the court agrees. However, if there are no further issues, I think that will just be a matter of waiting for the trial date to demonstrate that you have a safe, stable environment in which to care for Jeff. Oh, there is one condition, though. As long as you live on campus you could never move anyone else on campus without them being fully vetted through our background check program and being approved by the board."

He seemed to answer the questions as soon as the thought of them. It seemed perfect, but time would tell. "Ok She said." They had been sitting in from of the house she had shared with Jim for a few minutes now as the talked.

They worked out the details over the next few days.